A SAVAGE VALENTINE

ERICA AND DRAKE

NIQUE LUARKS

FOREWORD

Though you don't need to read my entire catalog to enjoy this stand-alone, you'll connect better with the characters if you go back and start from the beginning. If you've read a book by me, you know all the leading characters tie in together. Even if you don't read my earlier work first, but choose to after you read this, the order is...

A Heart Full of Lies (1-3)
    I Wanna Love Somebody (1-3)
    Covered in Your Love (1-2)
    I Give Him What the Streets Can't (1-2)
    You Set My Soul on Fire (1-2)

                    Happy Valentine's Day...

Copyright © 2018 by Nique Luarks
Published by Jessica Watkins Presents

All rights reserved, including the right of reproduction in whole or in part in any form. Without limiting the right under copyright reserved above, no part of this publication may be reproduced, stored in or introduced into a retrieval system, or transmitted, in any form by means (electronic, mechanical, photocopying, recording, or otherwise), without the prior written permission of the copyright owner.

This is a work of fiction. Names, characters, places and incidents are either the product of the author's imagination or are used fictitiously, and any resemblance to actual persons, living or dead, business establishments, events, or locales, is entirely coincidental.

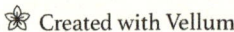 Created with Vellum

1

I GRAVITATE TO YOU

ERICA

I begged my big sister Erin to let me move in, and she finally agreed after I promised to get a part-time job. I hadn't graduated high school yet, but in two months, I would have my diploma. If nobody showed or acted like they were proud of me, Erin did. My sister was and would always be my biggest cheerleader. She motivated me to be better than her—even though in my eyes she was perfect—and she always gave me words of encouragement. Acknowledging even my smallest accomplishments. Even when I pissed her off.

My mother has three kids; Eli is the oldest at thirty, Erin is next at twenty-eight, and I'm the baby, just turning eighteen. My siblings look out for me regardless of whatever they're going through, and thankfully all I have to do is focus on school. I swore to Erin I would keep my head in the books. That's all she asked of me. I own a 2016 BMW thanks to Erin and get a weekly allowance from Eli that hits my bank account every Wednesday. I'm spoiled, but I'm grateful, even when I don't act like it. I go to school with people who can't even pay their senior dues, so even though some would consider me a brat, I respect and appreciate everything my brother and sister does for me.

The loud talking coming from downstairs peaked my interest, so I found myself climbing out of my California King sized bed and heading out of my room. Of course, I made sure my niece, Sanaa, was still snug underneath my covers. Her daddy was *thee* Santonio Keith Morris...aka "The Grim Reaper." People feared him...*a lot* of people actually. He was an urban legend to lil' niggas who wanted to be like him and girls who wanted to be with him. But my big sis has his heart on lock.

As I descended the grand staircase, loud music and even louder talking could be heard coming from the back of the house. My pink faux fur house shoes flopped loudly along the shiny marble floors as I ventured toward all the noise. When I got to Tone's man cave, I sucked in a deep breath and exhaled. Just as I was about to knock, I felt a strong presence behind me. It was like the room became still, the air thickened.

"What yo lil ass doing down here?" A deep, raspy, rough voice asked from behind me.

I turned around and he had to be at least eight inches taller than my 5'6 frame. He licked his pretty lips as he looked me up and down and then smirked.

My breaths were short as he eyed me. "I don't have to answer to you." Somehow, I found the strength to do something as simple as rolling my eyes. His whole aura was overpowering.

"Take yo ass on somewhere. Where the fuck the rest of your clothes?" Drake frowned, and then glanced down the hall.

I looked down at the white baby tee, and grey sweats I had on. I was fully clothed. Confused I stared at my hot pink toenails. Erin had taken me and Sanaa early to get a pedicure because her friend, Chance, was sick and couldn't link. Even though she used us as her back up plan, I was glad to get pampered for free.

"Excuse me?" I tried to ignore how fine this nigga was. Greenish, grey eyes, shiny three-hundred-sixty-degree waves that would make a professional diver nauseous, tattoos on his arms and a couple on his face. A permanent mean mug that was a little intimidating, and a few tiny scars, but it didn't take away from his soft, peanut butter complexion. He was decked out in so much jewelry I was sure any room he entered would suffer from a cold front.

His six foot plus frame inched towards me and I took a step back. "Take yo lil ass back upstairs." He glared at me.

"Or what?" I frowned. This was *my* sister's house. I didn't have to follow orders unless they came from her ... or Tone's scary ass.

Drake chuckled, grabbed my arm, and pushed me back down the hallway. "Don't yo fast ass got a test to study for or somethin'?"

I mugged him, and just as I was about to curse him out, the door to the den opened and Lucus, another one of Tone's cousins stepped out.

He eyed me, licked his plump lips, and smiled at me. "Sup, Erica."

"Hey." I replied dryly. Lucus wasn't ugly, or broke, but his smug attitude and arrogant demeanor was irritating. He was always lowkey flirting with me or saying something inappropriate.

Drake, who still had a hold of my arm, pulled me down the hall roughly. "Go upstairs."

I attempted to pull away from him to no avail. I was lost on why he felt the need to grab and pull on me like I was his child. Drake and I rarely ever said two words to each other. There were times when I felt invisible around him. So why was he doing all this now?

"I'm not playin' wit' you, Erica." He shoved me towards the stairs.

I looked at him like he had two heads. "You trippin'." He was handling me like I was his woman.

"Don't come yo ass back down here." He said before licking his lips and taking off back down the hall.

Asshole.

I climbed the stairs to finish studying for a test.

DRAKE

I made my way back down the hallway after getting rid of Erica. I don't know why she thought it was okay to prance around in tights and a half shirt. She was too thick to be walking around like that. I was gon' have a long talk with Erin about that shit. Yeah, she had sweats on, but that ass was still poking out, and I saw the way that nigga Lucus was looking at her.

I couldn't even front and act like I wasn't surprised he'd been checking her out. Erica was pretty as fuck. Dark brown, roundish-almond, shaped eyes, high cheek bones, and full pink lips drew you in immediately. Her skin was the color of honey. She was a dope little bitch, a lil' young, but no doubt sexy.

My lil' cousin Lucus smirked as I headed back to Tone's man cave. "You smashin' that?" he grinned.

"The fuck you just say?" I stopped in my tracks.

"I'm just sayin', she bad, if you don't fuck, I will."

Running my hand down my mouth, I chuckled. "Lucus ... I'ma only say this once. Leave her alone."

"Or what?" he challenged.

I snatched him up by his shirt and held his punk ass against the door.

"Dr-Drake...," he stuttered, "I was just playing, cuzzo."

"It look like I'm playin'?" I slammed his back against the wall.

"N-no." The fear in his eyes made me smirk.

"She off limits." I let him go and he almost lost his balance and fell.

I opened the door and stepped into the smoked filled room. It was so cloudy my eyes were burning from all the Kush being burnt. It was a Saturday night and instead of us getting fucked up at True's bar, we were chillin' at my cousin Tone's crib. The nigga was pussy whipped if you ask me. Him and his chick Erin had just come back from Greece a few days ago. They were only supposed to be vacationing but came back married.

"I'm 'bouta ride out." I approached Tone and gave him dap.

"Aight. I'ma get wit' you later, fam." He nodded.

After grabbing my coat, I tossed my chin up to everybody else, and exited back out of the room. I headed for the kitchen to get some food to snack on. As I made my way down the long hallway, I could hear my little cousin, Rome, talking. It was muffled like she was trying to whisper, then she paused and sucked her teeth real loud. When I rounded the corner the homie Royal and one of Tone's top goons, was heading in my direction.

He had a hard mug on his face, but he respectfully lifted his chin up. "'Sup, D."

"Wassup, young bull."

"I can't call it." He glanced back towards the kitchen, shook his head, and walked past me.

I entered the kitchen and Rome was sitting at the island. "What up, cuzzo?"

She shrugged. "Same ol'."

As I made my way to the fridge, I noticed she was coloring. "Big ass kid."

Rome chuckled. "Whatever. I'm bored."

Rome was Tone and Roman's baby sister. Shit was crazy, though, because they all shared the same daddy, *and* their mothers were sisters. Blood sisters that shared the same moms and pops. My auntie Macie was a scandalous bitch. I hadn't been out the pen long, but she had been on fuck shit since I touched down.

Rome usually stayed to herself. Just last month, she was living in Minnesota, working at a strip club; trying to keep the rent up on a crib in the projects. Last month she didn't know she had two brothers, and she hadn't ever met her mother up until recently. Now she was living on a guarded compound, surrounded by killers, dope dealers, and a crime boss. Baby girl was dealing with a lot.

After grabbing a water, I snatched a slice of pizza from out of the Pizza Hut box on the stove.

"RoRo, ride out with me. I wanna see if—" Erica's little hardheaded ass entered the kitchen and stopped mid-sentence when she saw me. She rolled her eyes and switched over to Rome. "Come ride with me to Tate's friend's house."

"I thought you broke up with him." Rome looked up at her.

Erica shrugged. "I did."

"Then why are you trying to pop on him, Erica?" Rome pushed the book away.

"Y'all don't need to be leaving this late anyway." I finished off my pizza. I unscrewed the cap to my water and then pointed at Erica. "I thought you had homework."

She smacked her shiny lips and turned her back to me. "Rome, come on before Erin wakes up and Tone notices we aren't here." She tried pulling Rome off the bar stool. "I just saw Royal and he's about to go to the liquor store, so we're good."

I went into my back pocket for my phone, pulled up Tone's number and pressed send. As I left the kitchen, he answered, and I made my way towards the front door.

"Wassup?"

"Aye, yo little sisters in the kitchen plottin' a great escape."

He chuckled. "Aight."

"Yep." I hung up the phone and continued to venture through my cuzzo's palace. I wasn't sure why hearing Erica talk about some other nigga bothered me. It wasn't like she was my bitch. She was a young, spoiled broad who whined to fuckin' much if you asked me. But she wasn't pullin' up on no nigga tonight; that I *did* know.

ROME

I didn't feel like leaving the house, but Erica kept bothering me about needing to see her on again, off again boyfriend, Tate. Erica could have any nigga she wanted, but she chased behind Tate's scandalous ass. Every other day she was crying over something he did, or mad about something fucked up he said. In my opinion, Erica let him get away with way too much. I knew it was because he took her virginity just a few months ago, though.

"I promise I'm not gon' stay long." Erica promised as her BMW coasted through traffic. "I just wanna ask him a question." She shrugged with both hands on her steering wheel.

I lit my blunt.

"I don't get how he can't answer the phone but is on Snapchat flexin'." She fussed.

"With who?" I exhaled slowly.

"Everybody, *but* me." Erica switched lanes abruptly and started cursing at a car that cut her off.

"I thought you broke up with him."

"That's not the point."

Okay.

I looked out my window. I wasn't in the mood for this high school shit. I was only nineteen, but even when I was in high school, I wasn't on this childish shit. If a nigga didn't want to be bothered, then leave him alone. Obviously, he got what he wanted now he was burnt out on her. Erica was acting like the shit was rocket science.

"I just know he better not try me when I get here."

I wanted to tell my sister-in-love she was wasting her time, but instead I relaxed into my seat and finished my blunt.

"Come outside, Tate." Erica put her phone on speaker and looked down at it.

"I just told you I'm laying down, Erica. I don't feel good."

I rolled my eyes.

"You was just on social media."

"And?"

"Well come open the door." Erica looked at me. "I need to talk to you."

I sighed.

Tate's end of the phone got quiet for a few seconds and then it sounded like he dropped his phone.

"Tate."

"Erica, I'ma just see you tomorrow, man."

I shook my head.

"Why tomorrow, when I'm right outside, Tate." Her tone hardened.

"Cause my stomach hurt." He huffed. "I don't feel like getting up and everybody is downstairs in the basement."

This nigga is full of shit.

"So ... one of your boys can't open the door?"

"Erica."

"Erica just hang up on his ass and let's go." I couldn't take anymore. "He ain't fuckin' with you like that, sis."

"Tell Rome to shut the fuck up!"

"You come tell me."

"Tate." Erica cut in. "I could've been in there talking to you instead of sitting in the car. I'm literally right outside." She whined. "You making me look desperate."

"Nah, you making yourself look desperate. I told you I don't feel good, so I'm not getting out of the bed."

I snatched Erica's phone out of her hand and pressed the end button.

"Rome!"

"Erica. Really?" I frowned, sliding her phone into my coat. "Why are you begging?"

"Give me my phone. I didn't come all the way here for nothing."

When I didn't budge, she popped the locks, opened her door, and got out. I reached into my crossbody bag and removed a strawberry swisher sweet pack. After opening it, I removed a pre-rolled blunt, and put flame to it. I watched as Erica knocked on the front door, took a step back, and waited for someone to open it. A few seconds passed by without an answer and she went to knock again.

For seven minutes I let this go on. I tried to wait it out, hoping Erica would read between the lines. I tried to be patient and see if Tate would call her back, but her phone sat quietly in my pocket the entire time. I took one more pull from my blunt and put it out. Then I got out of the car.

"Erica!" I slammed my door. "You doing too much." I completely understood the embarrassment she was probably feeling. But she was making it worse by standing outside in the freezing cold, banging on the door when nobody was going to come to it. Tate was playing her. And I was sure his friends were on the other side of the door laughing at her.

Erica chuckled before stepping off the porch. "Okay." She smiled wickedly. She walked calmly down the walkway, past me, and to the back of her car. "You wanna play?" She mumbled as the trunk lifted.

"What are you doing?" I asked from the sidewalk.

"You wanna play?" She said again. Erica emerged from behind her car with two cans of spray paint.

I snickered. "What the hell?"

She stormed past me cursing under her breath. I thought she was heading towards Tate's matte green Jeep, but she surprised me when she started back to the house.

I know this bitch ain't.

Erica shook up both cans as she climbed the porch steps. I took out my phone and recorded her crazy ass as she spray painted the entire front of the house. She didn't utter a word or stop until both cans were empty. After she was done, Erica stepped down to look at her handy work. Satisfied, she grabbed a decorative brick out of the yard.

"Fuck you!" She screamed throwing it hard at his windshield, cracking the glass.

I climbed back into her car and waited for her to get in. When she did, she started the car, put her seatbelt on, and took a deep breath.

She looked over at me calmly before pulling away from the curb. "Let's go to Town Topic. I want a burger."

ROYAL

"Look at these thotties." My boy, Waylon, pointed.

My eyes landed on a group of chicks.

"Hey Royal." A lil chick wearing a tight dress and thigh-high boots called out. She was the thickest in the group. Shorty had a pretty face, too.

I licked my lips and ushered for her to come to me. She quickly crossed the street and switched right to me.

"'Sup wit' you."

"Nothin'. Tryna get something to eat and get out of the cold. What you doing when you leave here?" She asked seductively with her head tilted to the side.

I tucked my hands into the pockets of my bubble vest and looked her over. "Shit, I was gon' hit yo line."

She giggled. "Oh yeah?"

I nodded.

"How? You don't even know my name." Shorty stepped closer.

"Tell me."

"Amelia"

"Put my number in your phone." I checked my surroundings as she went in her big ass purse.

"Ain't that that nigga Tone's people?" Waylon asked just as my eyes landed on Rome and Erica.

They hopped out of Erica's whip, talking. Rome dropped her phone and started cussing, causing Erica to laugh. Even in her glittery Ugg boots, and all back ensemble, Rome was bad. She was Chili from TLC chocolate. Rome was also on the skinny side, but that ass poked out something nice. Her eyes were always low and glossy cause she stayed high. She liked to play in makeup from time to time too, like today. She never had a lot on, but I did notice when she would go extra on her eyes.

Even without the makeup, though, Rome was rare. Her skin was soft as silk, her lashes were naturally long, and her lips were a perfect pink; plump as fuck too. She had high cheek bones, and deep dimples I would stick my finger in when she smiled. Her eyes were light brown and alluring; on some hypnotizing type of shit. Since I'd known her, she kept her hair in them long ass plait braids that damn near touched her booty.

"Okay, what's the number?" I forgot that fast about ole girl.

After running my number down, Amelia promised to call me when she got home. It was going on three in the morning, so I didn't understand why Rome wasn't at home. When I left there earlier, I told her ass to stay put. The only reason I let her off the hook was because I had heard Drake's footsteps before I saw him. I wasn't done with her sneaky ass.

Pretty soon Waylon's whip was surrounded by chicks and a few of the homies. It was cold outside, but nobody seemed to care. My eyes roamed the crowd a few times, but they always managed to end up staring at the entrance of Town Topic, waiting for Rome to come out. When she did, she was carrying a white paper bag and a Styrofoam cup.

"Rome!" I called out.

She looked directly at me, rolled her eyes, and kept on walking.

Oh, yeah?

I pushed off Waylon's whip and crossed the street in long strides. "You didn't hear me?"

Erica opened her door and looked back and forth between us.

Rome leaned against her door and crossed her arms. "What?"

I hovered over her. "The fuck you mean *what*? I told you to stay home."

When I wasn't driving Erin around, I was in the streets heavy. I didn't even wanna take the job. The fuck I look like chauffeuring. Tone sat me down after I rejected the position. He told me I was the only person besides him, he trusted with Erin's life when he wasn't around.

He offered to pay me double and told me I didn't have to do that "yes ma'am, no ma'am' bullshit. Erin was cool, though. She didn't ever really wanna go nowhere and she never really talked. As long as I got her from point A to point B safely, she was good. After nine at night she usually didn't need me.

Tone had the compound on lock down. So wasn't nobody coming and going between eleven at night and eight in the morning. My nigga had paid snipers guarding his family on some true boss shit. I didn't need all that power, just give me the money and a down ass chick.

Rome dug in her bag and removed a French fry. "Quit trying to check me like you're my man." She tilted her head. "Where is your baby mama?"

I knew she would go there. "Shit, I don't know."

She nodded.

My baby mama, Myka, and Rome didn't like each other. Me and Rome hadn't even been fuckin' around that long, but in a short amount of time, they managed to exchange more than a few words. It started with Myka going through my phone while I was sleep. She called Rome trippin' and ever since, it's been chaos. Nobody other than Erica knew about me and Rome. I didn't care either way, Rome was the one wanted to keep it a secret.

"Y'all need to go home, man." I opened her door.

"You got it boss." Rome hopped in and got comfortable in her seat. She faced forward and took a bite out her burger.

I stared at her profile wanting to check her, but not needing Erica in my business. I knew Rome was mad at me. Myka had been on good bullshit all week. Playing on her phone, having all her home girls add Rome and Erica on social media, only to inbox them talking shit. Rome wasn't the type to argue, Erica on the other end, was always ready to go to war.

"I'ma get wit' you later," I pulled gently at one of her braids when I saw she was ignoring me. "Aight?"

Still she ignored me.

Erica who was busy in her phone, sucked her teeth and looked over Rome. "Can you ride home with Royal? Tate wanna talk all of a sudden." She mumbled quietly.

Rome stopped eating and frowned. She finished chewing her bite, put her food back, and wiped her mouth down with a napkin. I stepped back so she could get out, and when she did, she didn't say nothing to Erica before she took off to Waylon's whip. I shut the door not bothering to ask Erica where she was going. Shit, a nigga was off duty.

2
I JUST WANT SOMEONE I CAN TRUST
ERICA

"Why the fuck would you spray paint my boy's house?" Tate yelled in my face the moment I stepped into his apartment he shared with his big sister. She was only twenty-five, but Tate made sure they had a nice place to lay their heads and nice cars to drive around in.

I looked around his living room. "I thought you didn't feel good." I walked towards the back. "You were too sick to come and open the door an hour ago, but well enough to get in your car and drive home?"

Tate ran his hand down his face in aggravation. Shit, if anybody should've been mad, it was me. Tate was a fine, chocolate nigga, with perfect teeth. He resembled Christian Combs, and he could dress his ass off like him, too. He was one of the school's star basketball players, which was why I was always arguing with bitches over him. He just had this certain aura about him that made you want to be around him ... be his friend. That was probably why I gave him my virginity two months into our relationship.

At first everything was cool, then all of a sudden Tate started acting brand new. We no longer went on movie dates, and long car rides. I couldn't even remember the last time we fell asleep on the phone. I felt like I was losing him. And I couldn't let that happen...

"Erica you lucky his peoples are cool. They not gon' make you pay for that shit." Tate dropped down onto his bed. "Then my car." He sighed.

"Why didn't you open the door?" I crossed my arms. "What were you doing? Who were you in the house with?" Tate was driving me to the point of insanity. He made me want to snatch my hair out and rock in a corner most days.

"I told you."

"You didn't tell me the truth, though." I shot back, aggravated.

"I did tell you the truth."

"Then why was Lauren sitting on your lap?!" That was the real reason I wanted to get to his teammates house so bad. I couldn't tell Rome or she wouldn't have come with me. Yeah me and Tate technically weren't together right now, but we *always* broke up.

Tate tossed his head back and closed his eyes. "All you wanna fuckin' do is argue, dawg. Why the fuck you so miserable?"

My head snapped back in disbelief. "*Miserable?*"

"Yeah. It's like you find reasons to be mad. I told you I was sick."

"But you're not no more?" I asked for clarification. Tate didn't look sick to me. He looked high and drunk, though. Smelled like cheap perfume too.

"I took some medicine."

I nodded. "You keep making me look stupid."

"Nah, you makin' yo'self look stupid. You keep accusing me of cheating and shit." He opened his eyes and looked up at the ceiling. "It's hard enough having one girl, having to deal with her bullshit." Tate dropped his head and stared at me. "Why would I want two?"

Nigga, what?

I frowned. "Well, you ain't gotta deal with my *bullshit* no more." My vision clouded from tears threatening to fall. "I'm out." I turned to leave. I didn't understand why Tate was treating me like this.

"Why you always overexaggerating?"

I stopped walking and faced him. "*I'm* overexaggerating?"

He lied about being sick, so I wouldn't come in his best friend's house. *He* was the one who posted video after video of him on Snapchat kicking it. *He* was the reason girls at school hated me so much. *He* constantly embarrassed me and made me feel like I wasn't good enough. But *I* was the one overexaggerating?

"Look, I don't want to argue wit' you." He sighed.

I nodded. "Okay, then don't." I started for the door again. I didn't want to leave, but it was clear Tate didn't want me to stay.

"Erica, I'm sorry for lying." He blurted. "I just wanted to hang with my boys. They had a couple of chicks over, but none of them were there for me. I promise."

I stopped walking again to look at him. "Then why couldn't you open the door or just come outside?"

"Because I knew you wanted to argue, and I was tryna chill." He got up from the bed. "You know you my baby."

I crossed my arms against my chest.

"You saw I came straight home after you flipped." His tall frame hovered over me. "I don't want you to be mad at me." Tate gripped my chin and lifted my head gently. "I love you, Erica. That's why I got something special planned for you for Valentine's Day." He smirked.

I sighed.

"You forgive me?" Tate planted a quick kiss on my lips. "Huh?"

I looked off. Was I stupid? Cause even though he pissed me off not even two hours ago, I was willing to forgive him.

"Erica." He kissed the tip of my nose. "You still love me?"

My eyes shifted back to his soft brown ones, and I smacked my lips. Of course, I still loved him. The real question was: Did he still love me?

ROME

I sat in the backseat of Waylon's jeep with my ear pods in. I couldn't believe Erica's dumb ass. He wouldn't even open the door for her; but his ass called, and she went running. What was crazy to me was how she and her big sister, Erin, were nothing alike. E loved my brother, but she would *never* let him disrespect her. Erin didn't even allow Toni to raise his voice at her.

It was going on almost four in the morning. The compound was usually on lock down during these hours, so I knew I was going to have to call Sadee. She was Tonio's mother and my auntie. Sick right? I knew even though she was sleep, she would come to the gate or let me in.

Royal: *I should be the one with attitude.*

After reading his texts, I looked up at the back of his head. I had every right to be mad at Royal. Not only was he still fuckin' his baby's mother, but the bitch was texting and calling me every other to day to remind me. It was my idea to keep things between Royal at a minimum, but that didn't give him the okay to keep messing with other people. I would never tell him that, though.

Instead I let him think I was mad about Myka leaving a long voicemail with her homegirls in the background. He didn't need to know I knew all about the chick from the club when he went out last weekend with my brothers and their crew. I wasn't going to tell him I'm friends with a chick on Instagram that uploaded a video of her sitting in the passenger seat of his car. Or the fact I saw the bird he was flirting with when me and Erica pulled up to Town Topic. No, I wasn't even gon' touch bases on the fact that Myka was telling everybody she was pregnant again.

Cause if I did that that would be admitting I cared. I'd been on my own all my life until Toni and Twin came and got me last month. I couldn't afford feelings like the ones Royal gave me. So, we fucked and only hung out occasionally.

I'm not sure when the shift in our relationship happened. Could've been the small things he did like going jogging with me every Tuesday and Thursday, sneaking into my room just to hear some of my poetry, or asking me throughout the day if I'd eaten. We never went on dates, and we never shared a kiss. But Royal was slowly becoming a problem. I thought about him way too much.

When we turned on the road that would lead us to the compound, I paused my music. I went to my call log and called Sadee. To my surprise she answered quickly.

"Rome? Are you okay?"

I nodded as if she could see me. "Yeah. I went out with a friend. You mind if I stay with you tonight?" Even if Tonio was sleep, he knew when the front door opened. It didn't matter that the master suite was far from the front of the house.

"Sure, I'll go unlock the door now and you just let yourself in." She said sweetly. "Don't forget to lock up, okay?"

"I won't." After hanging up the phone, I stared out of the window. My phone pinged.

Royal: Why are you so indecisive Rome?

Maybe I was. I changed my mind ... a lot. But that was only because I was used to nothing ever staying the same. I had been in so many different group homes it was ridiculous. I had become accustomed to just going with the flow.

When Waylon pulled up to the gate, Royal told him to put the car in park. He hopped out and opened my door. As I got out, security approached us.

"Who this?" He asked nodding to Waylon in the driver's seat.

"Family." Royal stared back at him, unmoved.

"I can't let you in here with him."

"I know." Royal looked down at me. "I'm just dropping the young lady off."

The security guard's, who's name plate said, Les, looked over his shoulder. He made some kind of signal with his hand and the gate slowly came apart. Les took one more glance at Waylon and headed back to his post. I grabbed my purse and glared up at Royal. I hated how sexy he was.

He had a soft chocolate complexed. Royal's eyes were piercing, but welcoming, at least to me. Thick, silky lashes hooded over them and his neat eyebrows were always in a furrowed state. His lips... Lord his lips looked so soft. On many occasions those luscious things had nibbled on my clit or sucked on my nipples. But they hardly ever formed into a smile. Royal's lining and fade were always on point, like he had just hopped out of the barber's chair. He was maybe four inches taller than my 5'7 frame and he was fit as fuck.

"We'll talk later." He eyed me. I knew it was more he wanted to say.

"Maybe we will." I shut the door and walked around him. "Maybe we won't."

DRAKE

I found myself at True's bar shooting pool with him and some nigga named Silas. I didn't trust dude. His eyes never matched his smile ... ever. A lil' bitch whose name I had forgot kept trying to get my attention. Every time I turned around, she was in my face, asking me if I needed anything. I needed for her stupid ass to leave me alone. And a nigga was two seconds from telling her just that.

True's bar usually closed 30-35 minutes before True felt like leaving. He did it to make sure everybody was gone before him and so he knew no one was outside when he left. The only thing with that was True wasn't ready to leave 'til five some mornings. I was a night owl myself, but that nigga could stay up for days at a time and still be on top of shit. He stayed with some lean in his cup too.

"I'm out." Silas spoke up. "Morgan ass been trippin' lately." He was referring to his wife.

"I don't know why you haven't divorced that bitch by now." A chick he had come in with rolled her eyes. "You don't even love her."

Silas shook his head but didn't check her ass. He dapped up True and then made his way to me. I looked down at his hand and then back up at him. He played it off by rubbing his hand along the back of his neck. I side stepped his punk ass and focused back on the game.

True laughed as Silas made his exit. "That nigga a straight bitch."

"On everything." I missed my shot and sucked my teeth.

~

Once the bar was cleared out, me and True kicked the shit in his office. It was homey as fuck for a nigga as hard as True. A nice red and black furniture set, was sitting off to the side with glass end tables. The silver lamps, picture frames, and decorations matched his desk. The shit didn't seem like some shit True came up with on his own.

"I need to figure out what the fuck Chance want for V-day." He mumbled. "Her spoiled ass don't even need nothing else." He scrolled through his phone.

I chuckled. "That's main?"

He frowned. "Main what? Headache? Bill?" True nodded. "Those two things, yeah."

"I thought shorty was it." I lit the blunt I had been holding.

"Nah, that's my homie."

I nodded.

Valentine's day didn't seem like that big of a deal to me. It was just another day where you had to buy a bitch a gift. Hoes already got anniversary, Christmas, and birthday presents. Why the fuck did they need another day for you to blow money on them. Shit seemed like a scam to me.

There was a light tap on the door. I frowned, pulling my piece from my side. The door opened and Roman, my cousin, stepped in. He had his chick Ava with him. Ava was fine as fuck, but she was family, so I wasn't even gon' go there.

"Wassup, nigga." True tossed his head back.

Roman approached me first and gave me dap. "What y'all niggas got up?" he asked as Ava took a seat in a chair that was in front of True's desk.

"Shit." True gave him pound. "'Sup, sis." He acknowledged Ava.

"What's up bro." She smiled. "What's goin' on Drake?"

"What it do Ava?" I nodded.

She shrugged sluggishly.

"Let's get a game goin'." Roman rubbed his hands together. "A nigga feelin' lucky."

"Nigga you always feelin' lucky." True laughed.

Roman chuckled. "'Cause I'm a lucky nigga." He looked to Ava. "Ain't that right, baby?" He winked at her.

She smiled, shaking her head. "That's right."

I smacked my lips at this soft ass nigga. Between him and that nigga Tone, I didn't know who was worse. Lovey dovey ass niggas.

"Bet." True nodded. "Aye, Av since you here, you can help me."

Roman took a seat on the sofa. "With what?"

True shook his head. "Ava can you tell ya guard dog to relax before I put him down."

"What's up?" She got up and took a seat on Roman's lap. "What is Chance trying to talk you into doing now?"

"I don't know what to get her for V-day. What is she into now?" He asked with a straight face. "Y'all be gossiping and shit."

"You know more about Chance than I do." She shrugged. "Get her some jewelry."

"Nah, Chance ain't into all that flashy shit."

"She likes to shop." Ava tried again. "Get her a gift card to her favorite clothing store."

True shook his head no. "I take her on shopping sprees all the time."

Ava snickered. "Well I don't know. What do *friends* get each other for Valentine's day?" She smirked.

True looked down at his phone. "I'ma just send her ass on vacation for the weekend. Will you go wit' her?" My nigga was really pressed over making sure Chance had a cool V-day.

This nigga whipped, too.

Ava smiled. "Plan it for the weekend after Valentine's day, and I'm down."

True nodded. "Cool."

"You niggas ready to lose some money?" Roman tapped Ava on the thigh and she got up. "A rack a game."

I stood up. "Nah, I'm out. I'ma catch you niggas later." I started for the door.

It seemed like every nigga I was surrounded by was letting some bitch make them soft. I didn't need that type of negative energy in my life.

ROYAL

"Where you been?" Myka didn't even let a nigga shut the door before she started going in.

"Myka. I ain't come here for all that." Sometimes when I didn't wanna drive all the way home, I crashed at her spot. Misa loved seeing me before she left for school anyways.

"It's almost seven in the morning, Royal. You should've just stayed where you were."

So, the bitch wanted me to sleep in the streets. I shook my head. Misa was gon' be up in a little while and I was taking her to breakfast. I just wanted to take a quick nap. When Myka stood over me as I got comfortable on the couch, I knew sleep wasn't in my near future.

"Myka Martin, leave me the fuck alone, man."

"If you were with that Rome bitch, I'ma embarrass her ass when I see her."

"Okay." Wasn't shit happening to Rome.

"You come here and sleep five days out of the week. She know that?"

Nope.

And she wasn't gon' find out either.

"Why the fuck you so worried about Rome?" From my understanding there was two other chicks Myka knew about. But she never brought them up in a conversation.

"Oh, so you disrespecting me now?" Myka inched closer. "How long you been fuckin' wit' this bitch, Royal?"

"None of your fuckin' business." I closed my eyes.

Whap!

A sharp pain shot through my bottom lip. I opened my eyes slowly and sat up straight. I chuckled a little in disbelief. Myka knew I wasn't into hitting on bitches. She knew I was still on papers until the end of the year, so she was trying her luck.

I rose up off the couch and she stumbled back a little.

"Royal, I—"

I slapped her dumb ass back causing her head to jerk hard.

Myka held her lip and looked back at me in shock. "You...you hit me!" She screamed. "Over her?!"

I snatched her up by her shirt as she cried.

"You want me kill you, Myka?" I asked calmly.

She shook her head no.

"'Cause I want to." I wrapped my hands around her throat. She was outta pocket for that stunt. I had known Myka for nine years, so she knew better.

"I'm sorry." She cried harder and I let her go.

"Take yo ass to bed." I stepped back. Myka had me wanting to commit a homicide. I snatched my jacket up. "I'm out, tell Misa I'll see her later."

"Royal, wait." She was on my heels. "I was wrong for that, we both were."

I swiped blood from my lip.

"Stay." She sighed.

I went to open the door and she jumped in front of it. "Myka, move, man." I wasn't trying to get no domestic abuse charge added to my already extensive rap sheet. Bitches like Myka were always a niggas' downfall. And my retarded ass went and made her my baby mama.

Reluctantly, she moved out of the way.

I was tired of these bitches and their mood swings. These hoes didn't know if they were coming or going, and a nigga didn't have enough patience to figure it out. I opened the door and stepped back into the cold. The was sun was starting to rise, which was perfect cause I had a few serves I had to take care of. Who needed sleep anyway?

Two and a half hours later I was back on Myka's porch. I didn't even let myself in like I usually did. Instead, I knocked and waited for her to answer. When she did, she still had that pink, silk scarf on her head. My baby mama was beautiful despite her fucked up attitude. She was what some would consider a BBW, but that shit didn't phase me.

She was always fly as fuck, her house was always clean, and she took good care of my daughter. Myka switched her hair up a lot too; I swear she had a wig for everyday of the week. She was almond complexed with a pretty smile, a phat ass, and some big ass titties. Myka knew she was fine, and niggas could cap all day about not being attracted to thicker chicks, but Myka had a whole line up of niggas who were willing to take care of her. The only thing ugly about Myka was her attitude.

"Go tell Misa I said let's go." I said and then quickly scanned the block.

She smacked her lips. "You don't wanna come in? I made breakfast."

"Nah."

Myka rolled her eyes, turned around and then switched away. Her robe matched her scarf, and I couldn't even front and act like her ass wasn't looking nice in the silk material. If she would've had some act right, I would've gladly blessed her with an early morning dick down. I shook my head cause I needed to quick nut. A couple minutes later Misa was running towards me, full speed, smiling.

"Hi Daddy!" She jumped into my arms and wrapped her arms around my neck.

"'Sup, mini me." I hugged her back. "You ready for school?" I asked putting her down. We didn't have time to stop and get food, plus Myka had already fed her.

"Mhm." She nodded, shaking the silver, black and clear beads in her hair. Misa swerved past me and took off to my whip.

Myka handed me the unicorn book bag that matched the bubble coat Misa was wearing. "They're having a Valentine's day party at her school Thursday. Parents are invited. Be there, please."

I nodded before walking off.

"Have a good day at school, Misa!" she called out. "Grandpa will pick you up from the bus stop."

"Okay!" Misa said as I popped the locks and opened her door. Once she was comfortable and in her seat belt we pulled off.

"Mini me." I looked at her through the rearview. "You havin' a party at school?"

She smiled, nodding. "Yep. They gon' have games and candy."

My daughter would be seven this year. Me and Myka had her when were sixteen. Back then when she told me she was pregnant, I knew I had to secure a future for both of them. Myka's dad, Mike, hated me, but when he saw how dedicated I was to my seed, he let me live a little.

"There better not be no boys there."

Misa giggled. "Boys are in my class, Daddy. They give girls gifts on Valentine's day."

"Somebody got you a gift?"

She smiled. "I don't know."

"You don't accept gifts from boys, Mini me, unless they come from me or Grandpa Mike. A'ight?"

"Okay." She cheesed and then looked down at her iPad.

I shook my head. Who the fuck told my daughter boys were supposed to give girls gifts on Valentine's day?

3

I HOPE YOU FIND YOUR WAY

ERICA

It was Erin's idea to have a girl's day. It was only me, her, and Rome because Chance still wasn't feeling good, and Ava was in New York. Sanaa and Toni were with our mom and Sadee had some errands to run. So, it was just us getting our nails done, sitting in silence. Rome hadn't said two words to me since the night we went to Town Topic. That was two days ago.

"Why y'all bein' so quiet?" Erin asked looking back and forth between us. I knew Erin would sense a disconnect. She was people savvy and observant as fuck.

"No reason." Rome said from behind us.

I smacked my lips. I had seen first-hand how Rome could cut someone off. She could talk to you all day for three days straight, laughing and joking, and then on the fourth day act like she didn't even know you're name. We had become really close, and I didn't want her to shut me out because she didn't agree with some of the decisions I made. I knew she was mad, but she was about to get over it.

"What's that for?" Erin stared at me.

"Rome is mad at me." I snitched.

"No, I'm not." She relaxed more in her seat. "You're a big girl, it's your life."

"What happened?" I knew Erin was about to nip it in the bud. "Stop being mad and talk it out."

I sighed. "It's Tate."

"Mmmm." Erin mumbled. "What about Tate?"

"He played me the other day."

Erin stared down at her hands. "And you let him?" She looked to Rome when I didn't say anything. "And she let him?"

Rome shrugged.

Erin sighed and then shook her head. "Erica what is it about this boy that you like so much?"

"Love." I corrected her. "I *love* Tate."

"Fair enough." She nodded. "What do you love so much about Tate?"

I watched intently as the nail tech shaped my nails. Why *did* I love Tate?

"Besides him being your first." Erin added curtly causing my cut my eyes at her.

"He listens to me." I got in defense mode. "He was there when everybody else was too busy for me."

"And now he's too busy for you." Rome threw in her two cents. "How ironic." She mumbled.

"Whatever. For your information, he's got something special planned for me for Valentine's Day." I smiled. "He knows things have been rocky."

"Erica..." Erin titled her head a little. "Is he hitting you?"

I was appalled, and Rome cracked up laughing, but Erin was dead ass serious.

"The way you talk sometimes be havin' me wondering if Tate's little punk ass is putting his hands on you. He's always dogging you, yet you're always vouching for him."

"No!" I shrieked and then looked around. "Did you really just ask me that?" I held my palm to my chest. "I'm not weak, Erin."

"I wasn't saying you were weak, Erica. I asked you a question."

"No, he's not hitting me." I couldn't believe she asked me that. "We argue, but nothing like that." I clarified. "Tate ain't stupid."

"Okay." Erin's hands rose in a mock surrender. "I was just making sure—"

"No need to!" I cut her off. "We're good. Like I said, he planned something special." All of a sudden, I wasn't in the mood to hear what Erin had to say or deal with Rome's sarcasm.

"Get out your feelings." Erin shook her head. "I was just showing concern. Jeanette was in an abusive relationship for a long time before we found out."

I nodded in understanding. I knew Jeanette was a soft spot for my sister. She felt like deep down she didn't do enough to help her. In my opinion, Erin had been a one of the best friends Jeanette could've had. But she beat herself up about what happened to her all the time.

"What's new wit' you?" Erin's gaze shifted to Rome.

"Nothing fo'real."

I smacked my lips again.

"Is that code for something?" Erin laughed.

"You might as well tell, E." I leaned back so I could get a clear few of Rome. "It ain't like she gon' say nothing."

"Say nothing to who?" Erin stared at Rome. "To Santonio?"

"Yep." I chirped.

"Okay." Erin looked down at her long, coffin shaped nails. "What's up? You having boy trouble's too?"

"Mhm." I mumbled.

"Damn, Erica." Rome rolled her eyes. "Tell all my business."

I shrugged. Rome was always bottling up her emotions. She was going to get grey hairs and worry lines before she was thirty if she kept that up. And I wasn't about to let her go out like that.

"Rome." Erin started. "It'll be just between us girls. I won't say anything to Santonio."

Rome closed her eyes and rested her head on the back of the massage chair since she was the only one getting a pedicure. "I've been having sex with Royal."

"*Royal?*" Erin asked. "As in my security Royal?"

"Mhm." Rome opened her eyes.

"When did this start?"

"A few days after I moved in." Rome pouted. For the first time since I'd known her, she looked sad. "He's got too much going on."

Erin nodded. "When I was you guy's age, I thought I was in love with TreVell. No matter what he did, I always forgave him, thinking he would learn from his mistakes." She chuckled. "He never did. Then Santonio came along."

She had my undivided attention. E was very secretive about the things she went through with Tone. I knew he cheated a lot when they first started dating, but there was more too it. They were a perfect match, but they had been through a lot of hurt. Looking at them now, you wouldn't even suspect they'd went through a period where they couldn't stand to even be in the same room.

"He wasn't perfect." She continued. "But I wasn't lookin' perfection. I was looking for somebody who loved me despite *my* imperfections. We went through a bunch of bullshit until we got it right. Now, I'm not saying that you have to forgive until it hurts. I'm telling you to always put your best interest first." Erin looked over to me. "We know when something or someone isn't for us." Her eyes rolled over to Rome. "Don't ignore the signs."

ROME

After we were done at the nail salon, Erin wanted to go shopping, so we ended up at the mall. She had drove her Charger, but Royal followed close behind. I had been close to him damn near all day and he hadn't said two words to me. While we shopped, he stood outside of the store, talking on the phone. Erica and Erin were deciding on Valentine's Day outfits, and I just wanted to go home and get lifted.

Once I felt like the store was becoming congested, I stepped out to get some arm room. Royal was standing with his back against the railing, staring at me. He licked his lips and then grabbed his crotch mannishly. I rolled my eyes and looked away. He was such an asshole.

Neither one of us had tried to reach out. He was mad and so was I. It was best if we didn't converse anyway. Apparently, we weren't compatible. I wasn't going to force something that wasn't there.

"Wassup wit' you?"

I looked up from my nails. My eyes connected with a handsome, light skinned dude. The piercing in his nose didn't take from his hard exterior. His dark brown eyes roamed my body and he smirked, showcasing a grill in his mouth. I glanced quickly at Royal and back at him.

"Is that how you approach women?"

He chuckled. "I was just trying to get your attention."

"Well you have it, so now what?"

Cutie licked his lips. "My name's Josiah." He held his hand out.

"Baby, you ready?" Royal draped his arm across my shoulder and kissed the side of my face. "Who's your friend?" He looked Josiah up and down.

Josiah frowned. "What's good, Royal."

"You know me?" Royal stood behind me and then wrapped his arms around my waist. He gave me a slight squeeze.

"Ya boy, Waylon, is my lil' cousin." Josiah eyes bounced back and forth from me to Royal. "You straight?"

Royal's grip on me became firmer. "Maintaining."

"Ah, yeah?" Josiah looked down at me. "I was just seeing what was up wit' an old friend."

I smirked.

"Stay up, shorty." He stepped back and walked away.

Royal let me go and I turned around to face him.

"Don't ever do that again." I mugged him.

"Do what?" He eyed me, looking all sexy and shit.

"Claim me."

"How the fuck you know that nigga?"

I gave him a blank stare as a response. I didn't have to answer to Royal, just like he didn't have to answer to me.

"You fuckin' him?"

"And if I am?"

The evil look in his eyes made me take a step back.

"Are you?"

"No!" I crossed my arms. "Even if I was, you're not my man." Myka needed to come collect her nigga. He was giving me a headache.

"Keep on." He mumbled.

"Rome you didn't see anything you liked?" Erin asked as she came out of the department store.

Royal stepped further away from me.

"No." Glancing quickly in Royal's direction, our eyes locked, then I looked back to Erin and Erica. "I'm going to Lush, I'll meet y'all at the food court." I walked off before they could intervene with my plans to be alone.

∽

Ten minutes into my me time in Lush, Royal walked in the store. Chicks were damn near tripping over one another to get a good look at him. I however, rolled my eyes and continued throwing cosmetics into my shopping bag. I was looking down at some "Sleepy Time" lotion when he came up behind me.

"What kind of store is this?" He asked taking the lotion out of my hand.

I snatched the bottle back from his rude ass. "Cosmetic." I then put a drop on the tip of my finger and rubbed it in. I did a quick smell test. "What you think?" Putting my finger his face, I waited for him to give me his opinion before I decided to purchase it.

Royal grabbed my wrist gently, and then smelled the lotion on my finger. He shrugged. "It's cool. What it do? Make you go to sleep?"

I nodded. "It's supposed to relax you." I went for another lotion.

"Give me this." Royal took the shopping bag from me. "You always shop here?"

"Yeah. Here and Bath & Body Works; I love their candles."

Royal nodded.

"Mhm, I'm about to call Myka right now." I heard from behind us. "This nigga is showing out."

I chuckled already seeing where this was heading. "Royal, I don't do drama."

"Me neither." He shrugged sniffing body wash. "This one will smell good on you." He tossed it into the bag.

"I'm about to FaceTime her now."

I looked back at the chick who wouldn't shut the fuck up. She was a big, burly looking bitch. Her weave was dry as fuck and her makeup looked caked on and cheap as hell. I smacked my lips and then looked up at Royal. He was too busy smelling different body soaps and lotions to see the irritation etched across my face.

"Royal. Who is she?" I pointed blatantly.

He looked over his shoulder. "Shit, I don't know." He handed me a small jug. "This smell like peppermint ice cream."

I took the face mask from him and opened it. After agreeing with him, I tossed it in the bag as well.

"She ain't answering." Big Bertha said loud enough for everybody in the store to hear.

I clenched my jaw muscles tight, so I wouldn't say anything, but she kept going. I faced her and Royal grabbed my hand.

"You ready?" he asked. "This bag getting heavy as fuck."

I looked down at all the shit he had thrown into *my* bag. "I'm not buying all of this." I sifted through everything.

Royal ignored me as we approached the counter. He sat the shopping bag down and the cashier began ringing everything up. As we waited for the total, Royal pulled me into his arms and hugged me tight.

"I hate when you mad at me."

My heart rate sped up. An uncomfortable feeling came over me. I tried to pull away from him, but he squeezed me tighter. "Royal."

"Hmm?" He sniffed my neck. "You smell like the PINK store."

I snickered. "What?"

With his face still in my neck, he nodded. "You smell like the inside of Victoria's Secret."

The chick behind us in line and the cashier giggled.

I knew I smelled good. I smoked a lot, but I loved the smell of perfume's and lotions. Just because I liked weed didn't mean I had to smell like it.

"$169.86." The cashier stated.

Royal let me go and faced her. He went into his pocket, removed a knot of cash, and peeled off three hundred dollars. After giving him his change, she handed me the bag. I led the way out of the store with Royal's hand on the small of my back.

"Since you're in a spending mood, I need some new panties." I looked over my shoulder and smirked at Bertha and her crew.

DRAKE

Auntie made Chili Mac, so I was posted in the kitchen with her, Roman, Rajon and Lucus. We were reminiscing about my little sister Deidra. I had been locked up most of Deidra's life, so it was nice hearing stories about her loyalty and the funny shit she used to do. Even my baby cousin Rajon, Roman's son, had nothing but good things to say about her. I regretted not getting to know her fully before she died.

After we were done eating, Auntie cleaned up as we let our food digest. Auntie Sadee was way different from my own mama and my other aunties. She cooked, cleaned, and read the bible and shit. Whenever Auntie was around, the atmosphere was chill. No yelling, cursing, or street talk. She was always smiling and always had something positive to say.

"Moms!" Erin yelled.

"In here." She called back.

Erin entered the kitchen with Erica and Rome trailing her. "I got you something at the mall." I looked down at the bags she was carrying.

"Oh, well, let's go to the living room and see what we got." She smiled, drying her hands off. Rome followed them. Erica was too busy in her phone.

"What you do today?"

The room went silent. I'm sure Roman was wondering what the fuck I was asking her that for, and Lucus was trying to see how this was gon' pan out. Shit, I didn't care what Erica's day consisted of, I just wanted to talk to her. Besides, bitches loved when you took interest in their day to day, right? She looked up from her phone and stared at me.

"You talking to me?" Erica looked confused, and then her gaze shied away from mine when my eyes never wavered from hers.

Roman got up from the table and then helped Rajon out of his seat. "I'ma get wit' you niggas later." He tossed his chin up and made his exit with Rajon running after him.

Lucus pushed his chair back. "I'll be outside when you ready."

I was riding shot gun with him today. I had a couple blocks to hit, so I was putting Lucus' hot headed ass to work. When he was gone too, I ran my hand across the top of my head.

"Come here."

Erica inched towards me. "What's up?"

"I asked you a question."

"I didn't know you were talking to me." She sat her phone down on the table and took a seat.

I nodded. "So, answer the question."

Erica's eyes searched mine for answers. She wanted to know why I was taking interest in her. She wanted to be sure she wasn't overthinking. I could see in the uncertainty in her eyes. "I went with Rome and Erin to get my nails done. Then we went to the mall."

"What you get at the mall?"

Her left eyebrow rose. She slumped back into her seat and the folded her arms. "A teddy to wear for Valentine's Day."

"Some lingerie?" I licked my lips and eyed her thighs. Yeah, I was sure Erica would look sexy as fuck in a teddy.

"Yep."

"What color?"

She giggled. "Why?"

"Cause I wanna know."

She rolled her eyes. "That's personal information, sir."

"So?"

Erica looked away bashfully. "Why you tryna be all in my personal business?" She faced me and challenged.

"'Cause I want us to be on a personal level." Shit, I was a grown ass man. Way mature then lil' Erica, but I wanted her. I knew my brashness was a lot for most, it was something she was going to have to get used to.

She stared at me. Eyes roamed my face in wonderment. Her head even tilted a little. I caught her by surprise. She didn't see this coming, and neither did I.

"I have a boyfriend."

"I don't wanna be your boyfriend, shorty." I gripped the seat of her chair and pulled her closer to me.

"Then what do you want?"

"I'm just tryna get to know you." I shrugged.

"There ain't much to know." She shrugged back. "I'm eighteen, I graduate this year, and my sister and your cousin are married."

"What that last part gotta do wit' me?" I knew exactly why she felt the need to voice that last part. But me and Erica weren't related, so she could dead that shit.

"Everything." She looked over her shoulder. "Erin would kill me."

"Why?" I pulled at one of her curls and it bounced back into a perfect spiral. "You grown, I'm grown." I leaned back in my chair. "I like your hair like that. It fits your face."

She smiled. "Thank you."

"No problem. How's school? Did you pass that test?"

Erica giggled. "How did you know I had a test?"

"I assume that's all school is about. Tests."

She smirked and nodded in agreement. "But I did pass." Erica boasted proudly. "Passed with an A minus."

I clapped, and she laughed at me. "That's what's up? You pretty and smart...." I licked my lips."

Erica grabbed her phone and stood up. "I'll see you later, Drake." She then hurried out of the kitchen.

I watched her until she disappeared. When she was out of sight, I snatched my phone up and left.

ROYAL

Waylon's mama's basement was full of niggas. We were leaving the block when he suggested we post up and shoot dice. I had my piece, so I wasn't trippin', but my eyes roamed the room every few seconds to make sure shit was still copacetic. Loud music bumped loudly as a few bitches danced around. I had a fresh blunt in my hand and a cup of D'usse by my feet.

When the basement door opened, I glanced to see who was coming down the steps. When I locked eyes with Myka, I already knew what type of time she was about to be on. She twisted in my direction, stopping a few times to talk to her home girls. When she finally got to my side, she crossed her arms and looked me up and down. I stared down at her lil' short ass unbothered.

"The fuck you lookin' at?" I finally asked her.

"A liar." She continued to mug me. "So, you took her shopping?"

"Myka. On my daughter if you get out of character, I'ma embarrass you."

She huffed like a little kid. "Royal, we need to talk."

"I'm busy." I fixed my eyes back on the d-game. "We can talk later."

Myka inched closer to me. "Royal, I'm pregnant."

I looked at her and frowned. "What?"

"Can we talk outside?"

I reached down to grab my cup. "I'm out." I addressed Waylon and then led the way back upstairs. When we stepped outside, I took a drink.

Myka stood at the landing of the porch steps and looked up at me. "I'm keeping it this time." She shoved her hands into her coat pocket.

"What happened to your birth control?" I wasn't trying to hear that.

Frowning, Myka shook her head. "Are you for real right now? I'm telling you I'm having your baby and you asking me about birth control? It's too late for all that." Myka sighed. "I wanna keep it, Royal." Her eyes watered.

"Man, you know we don't need another kid right now."

"Wow...." She sniffled. "What are we doing, Royal? You come to my house, layup, fuck and eat whenever you feel like it. I gotta hear rumors about you and other bitches, and take care of your daughter, but you don't want another kid with me?"

I shrugged. "Myka, you know what it is."

"No, I don't, Royal!" She wiped her face. "Tell me what the fuck it is!"

"Lower your voice." I warned her. I then looked up the block and then back down at her. "If I'm such a fucked up nigga, why would you wanna have another baby by me?"

"You know what..." She threw her hands up in defeat. "I'm keeping it whether you like it or not. I won't call you unless it has something to do with your kids, and don't call me unless you need to talk to Misa. Don't come to my house unannounced. Matter fact." Myka held her hand out. "Give me my key."

I took another drink of D'usse. Bitches were backwards. On one end she didn't want anything to do with me, but in that same breath she was saying she was keeping my baby. Wouldn't that make shit worse? Bringing another person into the equation?

"Is it because of Rome?"

"Why you keep throwing Rome's name around?"

"Because I know it's more to it than what you're telling me. You out showing public display of affection? Buying her shit? Since when did you start trickin' off on bitches?" Myka started climbing the steps like she wanted to fight.

"What me and Rome got goin on ain't got shit to do wit' you being pregnant, Myka." I had to remind her ass what the real issue was. As fucked up as it may be or sound, Myka couldn't keep that baby.

She chuckled and turned back around. "You're right. You wasn't shit before Misa was born and a new baby won't change that. You are selfish as fuck." Myka faced me. "This…" She pointed back and forth between us. "Is over. I'll get the money for the abortion from you tomorrow."

I watched as she stormed across the street to her car. When she pulled off, I finished the rest of the drink in my cup. I knew Myka was about to try and make my life miserable, but I was already living in hell. I tossed my cup in the trash bin that was on the porch, and then headed for my own ride. I prayed Myka didn't make me hurt her.

4

LETTING YOUR GUARD DOWN IS HONORABLE

ERICA

I had been at school four hours, but I was still tired like I had just woken up. I'd barely gotten any sleep the night before. Tate was acting funny again. But Valentine's was in two days and I was lookin forward to the surprise he had for me. Another reason I couldn't sleep, though, was because of Drake.

Him acting like he cared about my day kind of threw me for a loop. His ass was way too mannish for me. Drake walked like he had a big dick and knew how to use it. I didn't need those problems. I could barely keep up with Tate.

When the bell rang, I hopped up and grabbed my Ugg book bag off the floor. I didn't have any friends at school except my best friend Anais. We met eighth grade year and had been tight ever since. Chicks looked at my clothes and my car and automatically assumed I thought I was better than everyone else. Anais was the only female in the entire school, besides the staff, who didn't turn her nose up at me when I walked by.

"Best friend!" I was at my locker swapping my books out when she approached me.

"Why you are yelling like you ain't got no home training?" I laughed at her.

"Girl cause I'm in a good mood. You still linking tonight, right?"

I shrugged. "I don't know. I'ma see if Rome wants to come."

Anais rolled her eyes.

"What was all that for?" I hadn't known Rome for long, but I considered her close friend too.

"She's boring as fuck, Erica. She don't dance, drink, or turn up."

Anais was the party queen of our graduating class. Her dad was a truck driver and her mom a nurse, so she was at home alone a lot. It used to bother her, but now she using all the freedom to her advantage. Most parties happened at Anais' house. Hell, her house where I had lost my virginity.

"Rome ain't into all that." Which was weird because Rome worked in a strip club back in Minnesota.

Just when Anais was about to respond, someone came from behind me and slammed my locker door shut.

"What the fuck is your problem?" I spun around coming face to face with Kiara. She was Tate's ex-girlfriend and a mean ass bitch. Kiara was a cute girl, but her face was always turned up making her appear ugly. She stayed fighting or starting shit for no reason.

"I'ma just assume you haven't talked to Tate." Kiara smirked.

"And by the smell of your breath, I'ma assume you don't know what a mint is." I shot back getting a snicker out of Anais. I side stepped Kiara and this bitch shoved my head hard into the lockers.

I dropped my backpack and stole off on her dumb ass. We were going blow for blow and then one of Kiara's friends, Willow, jumped in. She yanked my hair hard, sending me falling onto my ass. Kiara used that as leverage to punch me in my face, leaving me dazed for a few seconds. Soon, two people turned into three and the next thing I knew Kiara's entire clique was either stomping or punching me.

"Break it up!"

I was still swinging wildly as someone grabbed a handful of my hair and yanked me across the floor.

"Enough!"

The kicks stopped, but someone still had a firm grip on my hair.

"Let me go!" I screamed out in agony. "Get the fuck off of me!" I couldn't believe these bitches were jumping me.

Finally, I was released and pulled up from the ground. Tears sprung from my eyes as I tried to recollect myself. There was hair, *my hair*, all over the floor. My shirt was ripped, and my head was pounding.

"Erica are you okay?" Anais reached for me and I snatched away from her. "Why are you mad at me?" She looked shocked.

I lunged at her and the school's security held onto me tighter.

"All you bitches got me fucked up!" I screamed, crying. "I swear to God! You too Anais!" I tried to break free from the tight hold he had me.

"Bougie bitch finally got that ass beat!" Kiara yelled from down the hall as our principal held onto her.

"Erica what did I do?" Anais asked picking up my backpack.

The security guard took it from her and dragged me down the hallway kicking and cursing.

ROME

Tonio: Come get this mut before I step on her.

At first, I didn't know what he was talking about. Then, I looked around my room and didn't see Grizzy B, my Bichon Frise puppy. I jumped out of bed and called Tonio's phone as I made my way through the house.

"Yeah..."

"Where are you?" I laughed. He was always threatening to do something to my damn dog. "If you harm one hair on Griselda we gon' fight."

He chuckled. "In my office."

I hung up and ventured through the mansion. It took me two and a half minutes to get to Tonio's office from my room; and I was speed walking. When I pushed open one of the double doors, Grizzy B was roaming freely around his office. His youngest daughter, Toni, was asleep in the sitting area. I stepped inside the massive room and trekked quietly towards him.

"What you tiptoein' for?" He shook his head.

I shrugged taking a seat in a free chair in front of his desk. "Didn't wanna wake Toni up." I knew first-hand how hard it was to get her to go back to sleep. "What you doing?"

"Going over some paperwork."

I nodded. I didn't know exactly what my brothers did, but they were caked the fuck up. Beautiful houses, nice cars, and expensive trips. When Erica graduated, we were all going to Maui for two weeks. She didn't know yet, but I was already bathing suit shopping for the both of us.

I didn't care how they made their money, I just wanted to get put on. In Minneapolis I wasn't living the best life, but I was maintaining. I always got it out the mud, it didn't matter that I was living in the projects at the time. I didn't like having to ask my brothers for money when I could be making my own.

"Did you think about what we talked about?" I pulled my legs up into the chair.

Tonio leaned forward on his elbows. "Yeah, I did."

"And?"

"I want you to go to school, Rome."

I sucked my teeth.

"Anything you need, I got you. Just focus on getting a degree." He tugged at his beard. "Associates, Bachelors, Masters, Doctorate..." He shrugged. "Pick one and we can start looking at schools."

"I don't wanna go to school, though." I frowned.

"Why?" His hazel eyes zoned in on mine; waiting for me to lie or come up with a weak excuse.

"Cause I'm not smart enough for school." I decided to just keep it real.

Tonio grimaced. "The fuck you mean you ain't smart?"

I shrugged. "I struggled all through high school. I barely graduated. And I only did because I was fuckin' the prin—"

"Aye..." He glared at me. "I don't wanna hear that shit."

"Well it's the truth." I shot back. "I don't wanna go to school." I didn't want my brother to look at me differently, but I wasn't book smart like Erica.

"Go for a year and if you don't like it..." He looked off in thought and then looked back at me. "I'll pay you to roll my blunts."

I laughed. "*What?*"

He nodded. "If you would rather be a blunt roller than the CEO of your own company one day, that's on you." He shrugged.

I sighed. "A blunt roller? Really? That's not a career."

"And neither is running dope or being a topless bottle girl."

I sunk into my seat.

"When you get some free time, write a list of careers you're interested in. How much you wanna make a year? What kind of hours do you wanna work? What kind of people do you wanna deal with?" He stared at me intently. "Set some short-term goals and then we'll start from there."

"And what if there ain't nothing I'm good at?" This was the first time someone took interest in my future and had expectations for me. The first time I felt like I didn't want to be a disappointment. 'Cause if I failed...then what?

"You a Morris, baby." He chuckled. "You're great at a lot of things. You just don't know your potential yet."

I smiled. "I'm one of the cuter versions of the Morris's, though." When he smacked his teeth, I laughed.

"On some real shit, you can be whatever you wanna be Rome. Just tell me what you want, and I got you."

The sincerity in his voice made me teary eyed. So, this was what it felt like to be loved. To be around people who were willing to go out of their way and wanted nothing but the best for you. Nothing was forced, and I never felt uncomfortable. I could get used to this.

For two and a half hours, I sat across from my brother and talked his head off. Mostly just about things like our favorite things to do, embarrassing moments, funniest things we'd ever seen, and my life in Minnesota. I opened up to him about my group home experiences, and even though his jaw flexed in anger a few times, he listened attentively. He told me he didn't like me sitting in my room, and then made me promise to chill with him from time to time. After I agreed, I scooped up Grizzy B on my way out. My big brother was a savage, but his heart was in the right place.

DRAKE

I had just got done fuckin' this little bitch I met at QuikTrip. After convincing her I was the realist nigga she ever met, she hopped in the whip and we went to the Marriot a few minutes down the highway. I pulled back up to the gas station thirty-minutes later and parked next to her car with my phone to my ear. Roman was telling me about this lil' nigga he had to pop. My cuzzo was usually a calm ass nigga.

Shorty removed her phone from her purse and cleared her throat. "I didn't get your number."

I shook my head when Roman said he put ole boys head in a toilet bowl full of shit.

"Did you hear me?" Shorty snapped.

I popped the locks and continued listening to Ro.

"Wow." She hopped out and slammed my door hard.

"D, I'ma hit you back." Roman yelled for somebody to come here. "These lil' nigga's think I'm playin'."

I tossed my phone into the passenger seat and got out. I had the munchies like a muthafucka. As I made my way into the store, I noticed Erica was at the gas pump. She was on the phone, talking loud, crying. I redirected my destination to see what was up.

"Erin, they jumped me." She sniffled. Her lip was busted, her left eye was damn near swollen shut, and her hair was in a messy ass ponytail.

I approached her, frowning. "Who jumped you?"

Tears slid down her cheeks. "That was Drake." She wiped her puffy face. "QuikTrip." Erica looked vulnerable and the shit was pissing me the fuck off. "Okay." She stared crying. "Bye."

"Who jumped you, Erica?"

"These bitches at school." She removed the nozzle from her gas tank. "Hating ass bitches." She put the cap on and closed the door.

I hovered over her and gripped her chin. I moved her head from side to side gently as I examined the damage. Each scratch, bruise, and gash made me madder. "Where they at?"

She shrugged. "I don't know."

"Why they do it?"

"It was my boyfriends ex-girlfriend."

"Call that nigga right now."

Erica looked confused. "Huh?"

"Call 'em."

"For what?"

"Because I told you to." I glared down at her little ass. Either she was gon' call ole boy or I was.

She huffed but started tapping her phone. Erica put the phone to her ear.

"Tate..." She sniffled.

I snatched her phone from her. "Wassup, youngin'?" I stepped closer to Erica.

"Who is this?"

"Aye, check it. Where them bitches at?"

"Bitches?"

"Yeah, the bitches who put they hands on shorty."

"I don't know what you talkin' about." He snapped, and I hung up.

"Where he stay?"

"Drake." Erica whined. "He didn't have anything to do with what happened."

"Man, look at yo fuckin' face!" I roared, and she flinched. Seeing her scared of me made me take a deep breath and a step back.

She stormed to the driver's seat and I was right on her heels. When she tried to get in, I snatched her towards me.

"What, you gon' hit me too?" She screamed in my face.

"What?" I let her go. "Nah—"

"Please let me go." She sniffled some more.

I sighed. "I ain't letting you drive like this."

"I'm fine." Erica snatched away from me and dropped down in the driver's seat. "I'm fine," she started crying. "I'm okay." She choked out.

"Man..." I drawled. All this crying shit wasn't gon' solve nothing. If she wanted results, then she needed to take me to that niggas house.

"I'm just so mad!" She yelled and then punched the steering wheel. "I swear to fuckin' God all them bitches gotta see me!"

I nodded. See, that's the shit I could get with. "A'ight then take me to ole boy and we'll figure the rest out, baby." Erica had me feeling overprotective as fuck. I was about to pistol whip niggas *and* bitches.

She shook her head no. "I'm going home. Erin is waiting on me."

I stared at her hard. Erica was too smart to be fuckin' with a nigga like that. It was obvious ole girl jumped her cause he was fuckin' off with her. I checked my surroundings, and then cleared my throat.

"Put my number in your phone, Erica." Now I was mad. She was protecting a nigga that didn't give a fuck about her.

I watched as she pulled up her dial pad and then ran my number down to her.

"Call me if you need me." I licked my lips. "A'ight? It don't matter what time it is."

Erica wiped her face again. "Okay."

I stared at her as she got herself together. When her face was dry, and she wasn't sniffling anymore, I closed her door.

"Pull up to a parking spot by the door."

A confused expression graced her face, but she nodded okay.

When she pulled off, I walked to the store and went inside. After getting a water and some aspirin, I paid and exited. Erica was still waiting on me when I stepped outside. She rolled down her window as I approached the driver's side.

"Here." I passed her the water and pills.

She took them from me. "Thank you."

I nodded before taking off to my ride.

ROYAL

"They what?" Rome yelled from the passenger seat of my ride.

We had just come back from the gym because I got a late start on my day.

"Erica." She paused with her phone glued to her ear. She tapped her foot repeatedly as she took a few deep breaths. "Them bitches jumped you?" She asked more calmly.

I came up on a stop light and looked over at her.

"Where was Anais?"

Rome's face dropped, and her eyebrows furrowed. "Oh yeah? Where she at now?"

I pulled off the same time she hung up the phone.

"Take me to the Starbucks in the Waldo area."

I frowned. "For what?"

She relaxed into her seat. "Because I asked you to."

"That's like a thirty-minute ride, Ma. I got shit I gotta do." I had to pick Misa up from her after school LINC program. She went every Tuesday, Wednesday, and Thursday because Myka's pops had physical therapy. He was always too tired to do anything else when he got done. Myka didn't get off work until eight tonight, so I was gon' take Misa to get something to eat and then drop her off with my parents.

"Then let me out and I'll catch an Uber." Rome started tapping on her phone.

I sucked my teeth. "What you need to go to Starbucks for, Rome?"

"Because Anais works there." She said flatly. "Erica got jumped by five bitches today and she stood there and watched."

Shaking my head, I hopped on the highway. "What the fuck they jump her for?"

"Over Tate's ass." Rome mumbled. "Just drop me off there and I'll find a way home, a'ight?"

I glanced at her. "Fuck you mean drop you off?" I wasn't dropping Rome off nowhere but home. I looked at the time on the dashboard and saw it was going on half past four. I had to get Misa by six. If I took Rome to Starbucks, then I wasn't gon' have time to run her all the way home and make it to Misa on time.

"Either you take me, or I can drive myself." She folded her arms. "Take me to my car."

∼

Rome didn't even let me pull into the parking space before she hopped out the whip. I grabbed my burner from the side of my seat, turned the car off and got out too. Tucking my gun, I followed her to the entrance of Starbucks, shaking my head at her. Even though she hadn't known Erica long, they were tight like blood sisters. I had never seen Rome so mad, she was usually the calm one out of the two.

We walked into the store and Rome stormed right up to a chick who was sweeping the floor. She didn't even say nothing, she just slugged the shit out of ole girl; sending her crashing into a table full of people.

"Oh my God!" A white lady jumped up from her seat and rushed towards the back.

"Bitch, you let my sister get jumped?" Rome screamed. She two pieced the chick and then snatched her up by her hair.

"Let me go!" Ole girl landed a punch, but it didn't seem to phase Rome at all.

One of the workers came from behind the register. "I'm calling the police!"

I held the door open for Rome as she drug chick out of the building.

"Let me go, Rome!" She cried. "That wasn't my fight!"

Rome wasn't trying to hear that shit. She punched her in the mouth, silencing her. "That's supposed to be your best friend!" She yanked her down the walkway.

I checked our surroundings knowing the five-oh was coming.

Rome let her go, and her dumb ass balled up in a fetal position. I watched as Rome bent down to untie one of her Air Max 97's. She removed it, wrapped the shoe strings around her hand and started hitting ole girl in the head with it.

This lil' nigga.

I snatched Rome up and carried her bridal style to my car. To my surprise, she let me without saying anything. I walked her to the passenger side, put her down and opened the door. When Rome got in, I shut her door, hopped in the whip and peeled off. I checked the time on the dash and seen it was quarter after five.

"I should've beat her ass with that broom." Rome grumbled as she slid her shoe back on.

I chuckled. "Your shoe, though?"

She shrugged. "It was the only thing within arm's reach."

I shook my head at her. "Yo lil' ass is wild."

"I never had a family to protect." She looked out of her window. "And now that I do, I'll go to war for them."

We rode in silence the entire way to Misa's school. When we got there, Rome looked over at me.

"I gotta pick my daughter up." I said, getting out of the car.

She nodded and then started fixing the bun on the top of her head.

After signing Misa out and making sure she had all her shit, I grabbed her backpack.

"You have a good day, Mini me?"

"Mhm." She mumbled trying to open up a piece of candy. "I was line leader."

I pushed open the door for her.

"Oh, yeah? That's wassup, Mini me."

Misa smiled up at me. "Daddy can we get nuggets?"

I nodded yes.

Once we got to my Audi A8, I opened the back door for Misa and helped her in. I tossed her book bag next to her.

"Hi." She waved at Rome. "My name is Misa."

Rome smiled back at her. "That's a pretty name. My name is Rome."

5

VALENTINE'S DAY

ERICA

I stood in the mirror looking at my reflection. The red body suit, and black, ripped, skinny jeans I had on, meshed well with my cargo jacket, and platform, high top vans. Since Kiara and her friends snatched a lot of my hair out, I had it in a loose bun. My eye was still red, and the scratches on my face were still red and sore, but there wasn't nothing a little makeup couldn't hide. I wanted to stay home, locked in my room, but Tate had been blowing my phone up all day.

After packing my teddy, and an overnight bag, I exited my room. Tone took Erin, Sanaa, and Toni to Disneyland, so the house was damn near empty and quiet. And Rome was in her room most likely high, listening to music. I knocked on her door and waited for her to answer. When she did, she was wearing a Nike sports bra and matching leggings.

"I'm about to go."

She frowned. "With Tate?"

"Yeah."

Rome shut the door in my face, and I stood there shocked. Ever since the day of my fight, she had been keeping her distance from me. I didn't understand why she was mad at me. Not bothering to even go there with her, I continued down the hallway and eventually out of the house. I hopped in my car and put Tink's "Different" on repeat.

After the fight at school, Tate swore up and down he wasn't still fucking with Kiara. Let him tell it he didn't know why her, and her home girls jumped on me. He promised he would handle her, but a huge part of me didn't believe him. Erin told me to cut him off, and I wanted to ... I *really* did, but I couldn't. Call me stupid, but I loved Tate.

I pulled up to The Raphael Hotel and valet hurried to open my door. I grabbed my bag out of the passenger seat and headed for the entrance. I pulled my phone out of my jacket and called Tate. When he didn't answer, I walked to the front desk. The man sitting behind it, looked me over and frowned.

"Can I help you?"

"Yes, um, can you tell me what room Tate Freeman is in?" I leaned against the counter as he typed on his computer.

"There is no Tate Freeman. Is there another name?" He looked over the top of his oval glasses at me.

"No." I shook my head. "Can you double check?" I called Tate back and he sent me to voicemail.

"Ma'am, there is no Tate Freeman. Would you like to book a room?"

I glanced around the lobby. "Uh ... can you give me a second?" He nodded as I took a few steps away. I tried calling Tate more time, and it went straight to voicemail again.

Is he for real?

I went to our text thread.

Me: *Where are you?*

I found a seat on a fancy sofa and waited for him to reply. For twenty minutes I stared at our text thread and didn't get a response. I got up from my seat and headed for the exit. It was hard keeping my emotions in while I waited for the valet to pull my car back around. I watched as couples all around me showed affection to one another.

When I was back in my car, I called Tate again. Again, it went to voicemail. The tears building in my eyes were more from frustration then they were sadness. I refused to believe Tate had stood me up. I went back to our text thread and seen he opened my message four minutes ago.

"But he can't pick up the phone..." I mumbled.

A car behind me honked and I guess that was my warning to move. I pulled off while calling Tate yet again. Each time he ignored my call, I got madder. I drove with no destination but ended up in front of Chance's loft. She lived in the area and I prayed she was home.

Just when I was about to call her, I noticed Drake and True walking through the parking garage. I sighed in relief and hopped out the car. Drake noticed me first. He stopped walking, said something to True, and then made his way to me. His eyes roamed me slowly when we finally neared each other.

"Wassup?" He licked his lips.

As usual Drake was wearing all black. Today he had on a black hoodie, a black bubble vest, black jeans, and grey Timbs. On his head was a grey skull cap. His jewelry was ridiculous. Several gold chains with iced out pendants hung from his neck. On his wrist was a watch covered in so many diamonds, I wasn't sure how he could tell time on it.

"Hey, is Channy here?"

He shook his head no. "Nah, she just left. What's wrong?"

I smacked my lips. "Did she say when she was gon' be back?"

"What's the matter?" He stepped closer to me.

"Nothing." I sighed in defeat.

"It's something." He wouldn't let up. "Why you not at home?"

The sound of a crazy stereo system made my eyes roll to True as he sped out of the garage. I guess Drake got tired of waiting for me to reply, because he spun around and walked off nonchalantly. I frowned and followed after him.

"I got stood up." I blurted. The shit was embarrassing, but Drake had seen me at my lowest already. When my face was red and swollen. When I was doing the ugly cry and my shirt was barely hanging on. Yet he didn't look at me differently.

He stopped walking and faced me.

"Tate stood me up." Saying it out loud put me in my feelings. Tate played me.

Drake stared down at me. When he didn't say anything, I crossed my arms against my chest.

"You judging me too?"

Instead of answering me, he turned back around and walked off.

"Get whatever you need out yo car and come on." Drake called over his shoulder.

ROME

When I shut the door in Erica's face I acted out of anger. I didn't understand why she was still chasing after Tate. Even after all that shit went down, the bitch nigga still could do no wrong. She was mad at everybody *except* him. I wanted to shake some sense into her.

But aye, who was I to judge? I called Royal and he rushed me off the phone after promising to call me right back. That was four hours ago. We didn't make any plans for Valentine's Day, but I at least wanted to talk to him for a few minutes. His funny acting ass was about to get put on the block list.

After making me a glass of wine, I made myself comfortable in the theatre room. Tonio had it set up like a legit AMC. There was a concession stand, a bar, and even a few arcade games. After a tough pick between 'Love Jones' and 'Just Wright', I decided to just watch both. It wasn't like I was doing shit else. I had two blunts sitting in the ashtray and the entire bottle of Erin's Château Margaux. I even popped me some popcorn and grabbed a bag of caramel M&Ms for when I got the munchies. It was the perfect setup for the perfect date, and I was all alone; then Grizzy B barked.

How pathetic.

I slumped back into my seat. Here I was judging Erica, but at least she had somebody that cared enough about her to do something special with her on Valentine's Day. 'Just Wright' started and I got comfortable underneath the blanket Sadee got me when she went to Vegas last weekend. I grabbed my phone.

I didn't want to call Royal again, but I couldn't stop thinking about him. I knew he was with another chick, though. I was convinced that's why I hadn't heard from him. Which was why I felt stupid because it was my idea not to put a title on us. I tossed my phone back into the seat next to me and grabbed the blunt and lighter out of the ashtray.

Halfway through my blunt, my phone rang. I ignored it the first time and then reached for it when it sounded off again. Royal's name flashed across the screen and I stared at it contemplating on pressing ignore. Why did it take him so long to get back to me? Did he think he could just fuck with me when he felt like it?

I watched the phone ring as I took a long toke. It stopped ringing and I grabbed my glass of wine. My eyes shifted back to the movie and I relaxed more into my seat. My phone went off again. I sat my glass in the cup holder and snatched it up.

Royal was Face Timing me this time. I answered the phone and reminded myself there was no need to have an attitude. Royal wasn't my man. We were just fucking. I didn't want his love, his time, or attention. He was just a fuck.

I had to remember that. Live by it.

At first his phone's connection was weak. Then, after a few seconds his baby mama came into view. I tilted my head in confusion, frowned in disbelief, and bit my tongue. Myka smiled into the camera. She fumbled with the phone a little and then her and her background became clearer.

"Hi, Rome." She waved. "What you doing girl?" She giggled.

I stared back blankly.

"I thought you might be looking for Royal." Myka laid on her side. When she did that, the camera landed on Royal who was on his back sleep. "He's sleeping right now, but when he wakes up, I'ma tell him to call you, okay?" she grinned.

I ended the call and dropped my phone on my lap. I sparked my blunt back up and focused back on the movie. But no matter how many times I hit the blunt, I couldn't shake the emotions surging through me. I never gave a nigga this much power; the power to hurt my feelings. If I was back in Minnesota this wouldn't have happened.

My phone pinged. Hesitantly, I reached for it again. It was a text from Royal that I knew was from Myka. Deciding to torture myself, I pressed on the message. When our thread opened, a picture of Royal, Myka, and Misa popped up.

She captioned it, 'Happy Valentine's Day'. I wanted to throw my phone, but instead, I squeezed it tight. I had to close my eyes, take a deep breath and exhale slowly. Had to remind myself that I couldn't let Myka take me out of character. If that was where Royal wanted to be, then I wasn't going to stand in his way.

DRAKE

Erica stared out of the window quietly. She hadn't even asked where we were going. When I told her to get her shit, she went to her car got a Chanel bag and hopped in the whip. She looked young and innocent with that bun and small amount of makeup on her face. Even though she looked like she was on the verge on crying, she was still beautiful.

Her lips were always shiny; I wanted to bite them muthafuckas. You could take one look at Erica and see she came from money. She didn't act like it, though. She was modest with her drip, but it was there. She looked down at her Apple Watch and then sighed sadly.

"What's wrong wit' you?" I asked, switching lanes.

Erica looked over at me. "I'm sad."

I chuckled. I never met someone so open and honest about their feelings. I respected that. Erica was straight forward. I turned the music down to give her my undivided attention.

"Why you sad?"

"Tate told me he planned something special for me today. He called me all day up until the time I left the house." She shook her head. "I get to the hotel and he didn't even answer the phone."

"Fuck him."

"That's the problem." Erica mumbled. "I did."

"Ah, so that's why you stuck on stupid."

Her head snapped in my direction. "What?"

"He took your virginity."

"I'm not stupid."

"In love…same thing." I shrugged.

"So, being in love is stupid?" She turned in her seat. "You've never been in love?"

"What for?" I glanced at her. "Love will get you killed."

"And pride will be the death of you." Erica shot back.

"I ain't tryna argue wit' you." I chuckled. "Don't take your bad day out on me." I joked.

"Haha…" She laughed sarcastically and faced forward. "So, you think I'm stupid?"

"I didn't say that."

"Basically, you did."

I shook my head. "How the fuck you gon' *basically* put words in my mouth?"

"You just said I'm stupid for being in love."

"No, I didn't. I said you was stuck on stupid."

"Same thing." She turned the music up.

I turned it back down. "Don't be disrespectful."

She pouted. "I didn't even get nothing for Valentine's Day. No card, no candy, a rose…nothing."

"What's so special about today?" I draped my arm across her headrest. "It's just another Thursday."

Erica smacked her lips. "Today is about showing someone you care for that you appreciate them. It's not about the gifts. But it is nice to be catered to for a day."

"Ain't that what birthdays are for?"

She laughed. "You stupid."

"So, it's okay to call me stupid. But when you thought I called you stupid you was finna cry." I shook my head.

She laughed some more. "It's not the same thing."

"Stupid is stupid."

Shrugging, she adjusted the heat. "Where are we going?"

"St. Louis."

"The Lou? For what?"

"I got some shit to take care of out there." I hadn't planned to take Erica with me, but seeing her feelings hurt in the parking garage, made me want her near me. I knew if she was in my presence she wouldn't have no reason to be sad.

"So, we won't get there until..." She looked at her watch again. "After five."

I nodded.

"Can we at least stop and get something to eat?"

"What you want?"

"I just seen a sign for an Italian restaurant a few exits down."

"Bougie ass." I smirked. "I thought you was gon' want chicken nuggets or a happy meal."

Erica laughed. "Did you just take a shot at my age? Okay, R. Kelly."

I frowned. "Don't play wit' me." Wasn't shit funny about being a pedophile. I didn't even holler at chicks who didn't look over twenty-one.

She cracked up laughing. "I'm eighteen, Drake I'll be nineteen this year. You ain't robbing the cradle. How old are you?"

"Twenty-six."

"Kinda figured you were, grown-grown." She smiled. "What did you go to jail for?"

"Armed robbery. I was supposed to get out sooner than I did, but I was getting into a lot of bullshit."

"Fighting?"

I nodded. "And a bunch of other shit."

"I got put in handcuffs once." She cheesed.

I chuckled. "For what?"

"Stealing."

"How did you get caught?"

"Anais got caught and they saw us come in together, so they stopped me too."

"Bad ass." I took the exit to the restaurant.

"You think it's going to be packed since it's Valentine's Day?" Erica asked, going through the songs on my phone.

I shrugged. "Even if it is, I'll get you a table. Whichever one you want."

She leaned onto the armrest. "You think they'll let me get a drink too?"

"Give a nigga an inch, and they take a mile." I shook my head.

Erica giggled. "I'm sad, remember?"

"Yo, lil' ass ain't sad."

She smiled. "Well, I'm not no more, but I was."

"That's all that matter." I pulled up to a stop sign and looked over at her.

She stared back at me. "I guess you right."

ROYAL

I opened my eyes and closed them right back. After Misa's party at school, she left with me and Myka. They went to get their feet and nails done and I crashed in Misa's bed. I had finally got some sleep after being up for nineteen hours. I rolled over and sat up on the side of the bed when my phone went off.

"Daddy!" Misa ran in her room and jumped into the bed. "My mama said she will be back."

I yawned and then stood up to stretch. "Where she go?"

"I don't know." She shrugged.

I reached for my phone to check the time.

5:43pm.

I rubbed my eyes as I made my way out of the room. I wasn't supposed to sleep for that long. "Put some shoes on, Mini me. We 'bouta ride out." I called over my shoulder, making my way through the house.

When I got to the kitchen, I grabbed a bottle of water out of the fridge and sat down at the kitchen table. I surfed through my call log so I could call Myka but stopped when I saw an outgoing FaceTime to Rome. I didn't remember hitting her up. I clicked on the call information.

Fuck.

I called Myka and waited for her to answer as I downed the water.

"Yes, baby daddy?"

"Why was you in my fuckin' phone?"

"What?" She tried to play dumb.

"Man, Myka, you gon' make me fuck you up."

"I don't know what you're talking about, Royal. I won't be back until like nine, so I guess that means you gotta sit in the house with Misa."

I hung up the phone.

"Mini me!" I got up from the table. "Let's roll."

～

Misa rode shot gun as I made a couple stops. When I was done, I dropped her off with my sister. I hadn't even bothered to try and call Rome yet. I didn't know what Myka had called and told her, but with my messy ass BM you never knew. That's why with help from Misa, I was just gon' pull up and surprise her with a few gifts.

It wasn't nothing major. Just a card, some candy, some candles from *Bath & Body Works* and a few items from *Lush*. And I convinced my sister to let me buy the red rose teddy bear one of her tricks bought her. When I got to the compound, I pulled up in front of the main house and parked. That nigga Tone was out of town, so I didn't have to worry about running into him.

I got everything out of the car and made my way to the door. I rang the doorbell and waited for Erica or Rome to come open it. Taking my phone out my pocket, I dialed Rome up.

"Hello."

"Come open the door."

"Why?" She didn't sound like she had an attitude. "Nobody is here but me."

"I know. I got something for you."

"I don't want it." Rome stated nonchalantly.

"Well, I want you to have it."

"Leave it on the porch."

I smacked my lips. "Yo, Rome. Come open this fuckin' door."

The line went silent and then she hung up in my face. I stood there for a minute looking stupid, holding a gift bag and a big ass, clear box with a fuckin' bear made out of roses. I shook my head and was about to sit the shit down, when I heard the locks on the door popping. Rome opened the door and stared back at me. Her eyes were red and low as she looked me over.

She tossed her long ass braids to the side and sighed. "What's all this?"

"Your V-day gifts." I smirked.

"I didn't get you nothing."

I shrugged. "This a woman's holiday."

We stood there staring at each other.

"You gon' move so I can come in?"

Rome stepped to the side and motioned for me to come on. Once I was inside, she shut the door and crossed her arms against her chest.

"Here." I handed her the gift bag.

She took it from me and went to sit on the right side of the grand staircase. Rome rummaged through the bag and removed the card first. She opened it, read it, rolled her eyes, and then mumbled...

"Thanks."

I nodded.

She reached back into the bag and took her time smelling the different shit I had got at *Lush,* and different scented candles. I let Misa pick majority of it.

"Thank you." She said again. "For the candy and the bear too." Rome looked up at me. "I appreciate it."

"No problem. It should be one more thing at the bottom." I approached her.

Rome dug in the bag and took out a white and gold journal. It was something I had seen at Target when I took my moms a couple days ago. I had planned on giving it to Rome just because, but it slipped my mind. On the front, in fancy gold calligraphy was 'Let the Mind

Roam.' I thought it was a dope wordplay on her name and the fact that she liked to write poetry.

Rome stared down at the journal and then flipped through the pages. A small smile tugged at the corner of her lips and then she looked up at me.

"I like it." She got up. "This was sweet of you." She tried to give me a church hug, but I wrapped my arms around her.

"Myka called you?"

"Mhm." She attempted to pull out of my grasp and failed. "Sent a family portrait too."

I frowned and let her go. "Let me see."

Rome grabbed her phone off the steps. She tapped on it a few times before passing it to me. I looked down at the picture of me, Misa and Myka. It was a picture we'd taken earlier at the school. I handed Rome her phone back.

"Misa had a Valentine's Day party at school and the parents were invited."

She nodded. "And afterwards you went and laid up with her?"

"With who? Myka?"

Rome stared at me. "Who else?"

"I wasn't laid up with her." I wasn't even rockin' with Myka like that no more. I decided that the night she told me she was pregnant.

"She FaceTimed me with you in the bed sleep." Rome's voice softened.

Her feeling are hurt.

"I was in Misa's bed."

She sucked her teeth. "Okay." Rome didn't believe me.

I went into my pocket for my phone and called my sister and Rome sat back down on the stairs. I eyed her as she flipped through the pages in her new journal.

"What?" My sister, Luna, answered.

"Let me talk to Misa." I put the phone on speaker.

"Misa! Your dad is on the phone." Luna yelled. "Royal, mama said call her."

"A'ight." I already knew what she wanted.

"Hi, Daddy." Misa got on the phone.

"Wassup, Mini me. You good over there wit' yo auntie?"

"Yes."

I nodded. "Mini me. When you and your mom went out, whose bed did I fall asleep in?"

Misa giggled. "Mine. I tried to wake you up to show you my nails."

Rome's body visibly relaxed. She bit down on the side of her lip and sighed.

"I'm sorry Mini me, I was tired."

"It's okay." She replied sweetly.

"I'll see you later, a'ight? I love you."

"Love you too, Daddy."

I waited for her to hang up before I gave Rome my attention again.

"You still mad at me?"

6

I JUST WANNA FEEL LOVED SOMETIMES...

ERICA

T hat night ... seven thirtyish

AFTER WE ATE, me and Drake hopped back on the highway. An hour into our drive, I convinced him to let me be deejay. I had a whole playlist with nothing but Beyoncé, Nicki Minaj, Rihanna, and Cardi B. Drake muted the music a few times because "his ears couldn't take it." Eventually he got high and stopped caring.

When we got to St. Louis, I thought I would've been tired from the car ride, but I was wide awake. Drake stopped at the liquor store and I hopped out to stretch my legs and get some candy. He held the door open for me as I entered the store. We went our separate ways as I went to look for Lifesaver's gummies.

When I saw they didn't have what I was looking for, I decided on just getting a Red Bull and some Skittles. I made my way to the front to see some chick smiling in Drake's face. She was cheesing all hard with a dreamy look in her eyes. I sat my items on the counter.

"I'm ready."

Drake looked down at me. "Go ahead and wait in the car."

I frowned. "For what?" I then looked back and forth between him and her.

"'Cause I told you to."

The chick smirked.

I chuckled at this disrespectful muthafucker. I mean, he wasn't my man, but come on... "Fine!" I snatched my Red Bull and skittles. "Hurry the hell up."

Once I was in his G-Wagon, I opened my Instagram app and scrolled down my timeline. My heart almost jumped out my chest when I saw Tate had uploaded a video. I hurriedly clicked on it and when it began playing, anger consumed me almost instantly. Tate was ignoring my calls but was at Anais's house. It looked like she was hosting a kickback.

Exiting out of the app, I went to me and Tate's text messages.

Me: You a bitch ass nigga. I'm not doing this with you no more. You don't really give a fuck about me. You never did. You don't have to worry about hearing from me again.

I pressed send and then looked out of my window and closed my eyes tight.

Don't cry.

I squeezed tighter.

That's what they want.

I opened my eyes again and Drake was coming out of the liquor store with ole girl still smiling in his face. She nodded at something he said and then switched away to a blue BMW. I watched with an attitude as Drake swaggered to the driver's side and hopped in. He shut the door and tossed the bag containing his alcohol in the backseat. I shook my head in disbelief as he started the car and pulled out of the parking lot.

"I'm so tired of you niggas." I stared straight ahead. "I fuckin' hate y'all."

Okay maybe I didn't hate Drake. I was mad at him, though.

"Yo ass need to take a nap." He glanced down at his phone.

"Why did you bring me here?" I stared at his profile. "What are we doing?"

Drake ignored me as he coasted through traffic with Tupac blasting. When I noticed he wasn't going to give me a response, I faced forward and got back on social media. Everybody was celebrating their Valentine's Day all happy and shit. Giving and receiving gifts and I was riding shot gun with a nigga that just exchanged numbers with a bitch inside of a liquor store. Yeah, I was big mad. Even Erin was in California living her best life and Rome had uploaded a picture of things I'm sure Royal had gifted her.

After going on a liking spree, I dropped my phone into my lap. I looked out my window in defeat. I just wanted the day to be over. When I woke up this morning, you couldn't have paid me to believe this was how my day was going to end. I officially hated Valentine's Day.

Twenty minutes later, Drake pulled up in a shopping center that looked like it was about to close. He parked in front of a jewelry store, put his phone to his ear and got out. I followed his lead, making sure to slam my door extra hard. I didn't give a damn about the look he was giving me as I switched past him. I stopped in front of the door and looked back at Drake.

"They're closed."

He stood behind me protectively. "Shit, I won't be back to the city until morning." Drake said to whoever he was on the phone with. "Tell that lil' nigga I don't give a fuck. He got sixty seconds to bring you that."

A man inside the store approached the door with a ring of keys in his hand and a smile on his face.

"I'ma call you back."

The Arabian man on the other side of the glass unlocked the door and let us inside.

"Drake, buddy." He grinned.

"What's good, Fab." They exchanged handshakes.

We then followed Fab to the back of the store.

"I was wondering when I would see you for a new piece." He

unlocked another door that led us into a fancy room. "Make yourself comfortable." He nodded towards me.

I stayed out right next to Drake.

"I know you tryna get home to the wife." Drake guided me by the small of my back to a fancy oak table. "So, we won't be long." He pulled out a chair for me to sit down.

"Water, juice, champagne?" Fab asked me.

I shook my head no as I took a seat.

He nodded and then looked to Drake. "So, what can I get you? A new watch, a pendant?"

Drake sat down. "What you want?" He stared at me.

"Huh?" I asked confused.

Drake looked back up at Fab. "Let me see your tennis bracelets."

ROME

After Royal showed up with those gifts for me, it was hard to stay mad at him. We wound up in my room, lying across my bed. The lamp on my dresser and the few candles I lit gave the room a relaxed feel. That mixed with my 'The Weeknd' Pandora station playing lowly from the speakers throughout the room. We laid face to face vibing.

"Why are you looking at me like that?" I snuggled with my pillow.

"Just thinking."

"About?"

"Why you like being cooped up in this house." Royal moved one of my braids out of my face.

I shrugged. "What's there to do outside?" I didn't do the club scene, unless I was getting paid, and Erica wasn't here for me to explore the city with someone. I liked being at home. I had everything I needed at my disposal.

"It's a lot to do."

"Mmmm."

He wrapped his arm around me.

"It's like you hiding from the world. Why?" Royal stared into my eyes. "You're beautiful and fly as fuck. Chicks that look like you become Instagram models and shit." He joked, and I rolled my eyes.

"That was shallow. And I'm not hiding from the world, I'm working on me. I can't do that flexing on social media." I informed him. "There's so much more to me than just the way that I look, Royal."

"I know." He licked his lips.

I sighed softly. "I like being alone. When I'm by myself, I don't have to worry about offending nobody. People are so sensitive nowadays." I ran my thumb gently across his eyebrow and the muscles in his face relaxed. "It's easier to just stay in my own lane...ya know?"

He nodded. "You just gotta surround yourself with like-minded people."

"I don't have time for that. I'm still trying to figure out what I wanna do with my life. I'll be twenty this year. I need to be setting some form of foundation for my future."

"You on the right path, Rome. You different. Especially for a young chick. You don't sit in the mirror all day putting on makeup and shit. Instead of hitting up the club with a fake ID hollering 'aye' half naked, you would rather sit around the house writing your feelings down."

I stared into his eyes.

"Ain't nothing wrong with that." Royal caressed my thigh.

I inched closer to him. "You're cute when you're not being an asshole."

He chuckled. "You cute either way."

I felt my cheeks get hot.

"Pretty ass." He gripped my chin. "You mine." Royal then pulled me in for a kiss.

At first, I hesitated. Kissing went against my rules. It was an intimate form of affection. To me, it meant I was being too vulnerable. But I grabbed the side of Royal's face and deepened our first kiss.

His lips were so soft. His tongue tasted like mint. Royal climbed on top of me, still kissing and sucking my lips. He raised my arms over my head and trailed soft kisses down my chin, and then kissed the large red rose on the front of my neck. I moaned when his tongue slid down the middle of my chest.

He let go of my hands, and slowly slid my leggings and my panties down my legs. Once they were completely off, he kissed the inside of my thighs. A tingling sensation shot through my limbs when his tongue flicked across my nub. Royal wet my clit up as his licks sped up. When I started squirming, he held on tight to my thighs.

"Sss..." my eyes rolled to the back of head. "Royal." I could feel my clit growing.

When he moaned into my love, I grabbed the back of his head. His spit trickled down the crack of my ass. Royal then slid his finger into my pussy. Between the music playing, him moaning, and devouring my sex, I didn't know how much longer I was going to last. I didn't have to wonder for long, though.

When he slipped a second finger in me and fucked me harder, my eyes shot open.

"Oh...my...God." The top half of my body rose. "Royal..." That last lick was it.

I came so hard my body froze momentarily. Royal kept licking, sucking, and finger fucking me. A numbness came over me and a chill crept down my spine. For a minute I legit thought I was paralyzed. I tried to push his head away, but he wouldn't move.

"Royal." I moaned. "Wait."

But he didn't. Instead he sped up. He ate my pussy so good, I fell flat on my back and just surrendered. A second orgasm crept up on me a few seconds later. It hit me so hard, the last thing I remembered was calling out to God.

DRAKE

"Ice me out, nigga... Ice me out." Erica rapped along to some song she had put on replay for the last twenty minutes as she recorded a video. She put the camera on me, rapping word from word.

I shook my head at her flexing ass.

She ended up getting a diamond studded Rollie, tennis bracelet, *and* necklace. Lil spoiled ass cheesed the whole time I was cashing Fab out. I had never spent that much money on a chick but seeing Erica smile was like a drug. The shit was addictive and satisfying as fuck.

She turned down the music as I lit my blunt. "He match my fly." Erica turned the camera back on me and I threw up my hood.

My phone sounded off. "Cuzzo."

"Put Erica on the phone!" Erin blasted into my ear. I knew it was her because she was the only chick that would have Tone's phone.

I passed my phone to Erica and she sucked her teeth. "Hello." She continued smiling into the camera. "Happy Valentine's Day to you too, sister." She paused. "I'm in St. Louis." Erica laughed. "So, if you can see me on Facebook live, then why are you calling me?"

I looked over at her.

"I love you sister, I'ma call you when I get off live." She passed me my phone.

I saw the time was still running, so I put the phone back to my ear. "Yeah."

"Man, what the fuck are you doin' wit' Erica's young ass?"

I took a pull from my blunt and exhaled from my nostrils. "We chillin'."

"Yeah, a'ight. You gettin' me cussed the fuck out."

"Tell E's mean ass it ain't even nothing like that."

"This why you hoes mad and wanna jump me and shit." Erica spoke into the phone, still on Facebook live. "Hey, cousin. Yes, girl I got bitches bothered." She laughed.

"You wild. I'ma get wit' you later."

I hung up the phone and dropped into my lap.

"Get off Facebook." I licked my lips.

Erica fake pouted. "I'll talk to y'all later. Happy Valentine's Day."

"You hungry?"

She nodded as she relaxed into her seat. "I'm sleepy too. I had an emotional day."

I nodded. "A'ight. I'ma take you to get something to eat and then drop you off at the room."

Her head snapped in my direction. "Where are you going?"

"I got some shit I gotta handle."

"Niggas..." she mumbled.

∼

I dropped off Erica so I could link with my boys from the Northside. Tone did a lot of business with the cats out here. Since he was taking over shit for Don Capporelli, he couldn't move around like he used to. That's why I was here in his place. They owed, and I came to collect. The exchange happened in less ten minutes and then I was on my way.

I decided to just go back to the room since Erica was there waiting on me. I figured while she slept, I could count money, that way I knew everything was everything before we headed back to Kansas City. After grabbing the duffle bag and the sack from the liquor store, I made my way inside Moonrise Hotel. The hotel had a rooftop bar that I was gon' check out when I got done counting up. If Erica's little angry ass acted right she could come with me.

I let myself in the room and Erica was asleep in the bed. She was still wearing her ice. I tossed the duffle bag on the floor wondering how a person could sleep pretty. I had to take a seat on the bed and listen for her breathing because she was barely moving. I moved her hair out of her face and stared down at her.

I put the liquor bag on the dresser and took my phone out of my bubble vest. I snapped a quick picture of her. When she stirred I got up from the bed and went to take a leak. I was washing my hands when there was a knock on the door.

"Wassup?"

"I was just making sure that was you." Erica said from the other side of the door.

"Who else would it be, Ma." Shaking my head, I dried my hands off.

"Did you know there was a rooftop bar?" She asked as I opened the door.

"I nodded."

"We should go."

I removed my vest and tossed it on the bed before I sat down. "You ain't even old enough to drink."

"So? I have a fake ID."

Good. I planned on taking her up there anyways. Now I didn't have to bribe nobody.

"We can go after I get done doing this."

She nodded before heading into the bathroom.

I reached for the duffel bag and started removing neat stacks of cash. After I emptied out the bag, I grabbed the liquor off the night stand. I drank a few times from the Remy bottle and then began counting up. The bathroom door opened, and Erica stepped out. My back was to her when she asked...

"Can you take my picture? I need a full body pic before I take this off."

"Gimme a minute."

"Why can't you do it now?"

"'Cause I'm busy."

She dropped onto the bed next to me. "That's a lot of money. Did you rob someone?"

"What?" I frowned. "I'ma killer, Ma... not a thief."

Her eyes widened. "That's worse!"

"You're entitled to your opinion." I was a lot of things, but stealing was like snitching to me.

"You're crazy." Erica mumbled.

"I know." I looked over at her. "I'm cool wit' that, though."

"If you like it, then I love it." She shrugged. "I know what Eli does. Tone too." She paused. "Well, I don't know *exactly* what they do, but I know it's illegal."

I focused on counting.

"So, where's your girlfriend?" Erica reached around me for the bottle of Remy. "At home with your kids?"

I chuckled, still counting. "You've known me for how long? When have you ever seen me come around with shorties?"

"Thought maybe you had one of those bitter baby mama's."

I laughed, and she took a baby sip from the bottle.

"So, are you going to try and fuck me?"

I faced her.

"I mean. You fed me twice today. Loved that Italian restaurant by the way." Erica took another sip. "You bought me jewelry. Now, we're in a nice ass hotel."

"I didn't do none of that to get the pussy, kid." I continued to stare at her. "I ain't hurting for coochie."

She laughed. "*Coochie?* That's a gross word."

I chuckled and went back to counting.

"Thanks again, Drake."

"For what?"

"Being nice to me today. Making my Valentine's Day rememberable. Tate played the fuck outta me." She said sadly. "He's been uploading shit all day." She took another small sip. "Bastard."

I finished counting up and zipped the bag and then I grabbed my vest.

Erica jumped up. "Can you still take my picture?" She tried to hand me her phone.

I grabbed mine off the bed and went to my camera. "Come on."

ROYAL

Rome passed out in the middle of me eating her pussy. Shorty was still knocked too. She was laid up underneath me, snoring. I was about to close my eyes and take another quick nap when my phone sounded off. Seeing Myka's name made me shake my head.

Myka: Why did you drop Misa off with Luna?
Me: Had some shit to take care of
Myka: She said you bought candy and shit.
Me: Ok.
Myka: For who? Cause when I got home there was nothing here.
Me: Why Myka?
Myka: You sho right Royal. I'm done fuckin with you
Me: Ok

I was done fuckin' with her ass too. I tossed my phone to the side of me and pulled Rome closer to me. A part of me wanted to slide up in her, but I wasn't even gon' disrespect Tone like that. We never fucked in his house and I wasn't about to start now just because he was out of town. Just when I shut my eyes, Rome's phone started ringing.

I grabbed it, seen it was an unknown number, and pressed ignore. I stared down at Rome. She had me fucked up. I was on some sucker shit, eating pussy, and she had niggas blowing her phone up. She scooted closer to me, still snoring. I was about to wake her ass up and then her phone went off again.

This time it was a FaceTime. I answered, still leaning over her sideways. When she moved again, I looked down at her, frowning.

"Royal?" The caller said my name.

They came into clear view and I didn't recognize them. "Who you?" Me and Rome didn't know the same people.

"Oh shit!" She said excitedly. "Biiitch..." She drawled. "Here."

I glanced back down at Rome as the caller passed the phone off. When Myka got in the camera, I sucked my teeth.

"For real, Royal?" She grilled me. "You dropped your daughter off to go and lay up with a bitch!"

"Why are you playing on her phone?"

"Nigga, fuck you."

I lowered the volume on the phone when Rome stirred. I put the camera on my baby.

"She sleep, what y'all want?"

Myka hung up in my face and I blocked the number. I would deal with my BM later. I tossed Rome's phone next to mine and then pulled her into my chest. I wanted to enjoy just a little bit of peace before I jumped into traffic. Being with Rome was just that; peaceful as fuck.

7
STRATEGY IS BETTER THAN STRENGTH
ERICA

I had a banging ass headache when I opened my eyes. Thank God the room was pitch black; the darkness not only helped with the pain, but it made it easier to adjust my tired eyes. I squinted a little as I felt around for my phone. When I felt a body instead, I scooted closer to it. I patted the figure until I touched a huge bulge and then they grabbed my wrist.

"Why you feelin' me up." Drake grumbled: "Keep your lil' freaky ass over there."

I quickly pulled my arm away. "Turn the light on."

"You turn it on." He mumbled. "Why the fuck you always giving orders like a nigga the help or somethin'?"

I held the side of my head as I giggled softly. "I can't see anything."

Drake moved around, then I heard a click and the lamp next to him came on. The light illuminated the room and I was finally able to see. Drake was sitting up on the side of the bed, his entire back was decorated in tattoos. Polo briefs hugged his waist. That's when I looked down at my own body and saw I was in nothing but my black lace bra and panties.

"Did we..."

"Nah." He answered with his back still to me.

I nodded. "My head hurts." I dropped my head back onto the soft, fluffy pillow. "What time is it?"

"Nine." He passed me my phone.

I took it from him and saw I had twenty missed calls from Tate, one from Erin, two from Rome, and six from my mom. "Shit." I dialed my mom first.

"Erica Chanel..."

I rolled my eyes.

"Where the hell have you been?" She yelled like it wasn't nine o'clock in the morning. "Your grandma said you were on Facebook with some man."

Damn, I thought I blocked her old ass.

I glanced at Drake. His back was still to me.

"I'm in St. Louis."

"With who? The man with those tattoos on his face? Yeah, your grandmother told me. Get your ass home, now!"

I frowned. "I don't even live with you."

"I don't give a damn! Why didn't you tell me you were suspended? Ever since you moved in with Erin, you've been smelling yourself. Bring your ass home ... today!" She hung up in my face.

"I swear she get on my fuckin' nerves." I called Erin next. "I'm not a baby." I said to myself as I tossed the covers off me.

Drake chuckled, making his way to the bathroom.

"Your mama is looking for you." Erin yawned into the phone.

I smacked my lips. "I know, I just got off the phone with her. She's tripping."

"Why are you with Drake, Erica? When did y'all start fuckin' around?"

"We're not fuckin'. Tate stood me up and I ran into him. He saw I was down and offered to spend the day with me." I tried to act like it wasn't nothing, but my day with Drake been the best one I'd had in a long time. I didn't have to spend one dollar, I got gifts, and he let me get drunk with him.

"But he bought you all that jewelry?"

I looked down at the tennis bracelet on my wrist. I then pulled gently at the tennis necklace. "It was Valentine's Day."

Erin smacked her lips. "Erica, you're eighteen so you're going to do what you want. Tell Drake, I fight niggas too."

I laughed. That's why I loved my big sister. She was my ride or die, right or wrong. "I'll call you when you get back to the house. Kiss Naa and Toni for me."

"Okay, later."

"Later."

I figured since I would see Rome in a couple hours, I would talk to her then. And knowing Rome, she probably wasn't up. Her ass was not a morning person. The house could be on fire, but if it was too early Rome would be ready and willing to meet her maker. It didn't matter what time she went to bed.

Drake exited the bathroom with his phone to his ear. My eyes dropped down to his pelvic area and I absentmindedly licked my lips. He wasn't paying me any mind as I eyed his sexy ass. I climbed out of bed and went for my overnight bag. Being half naked around Drake was a recipe for disaster.

"Yeah, let me hit you back." He told his caller as I passed him.

I entered the bathroom and shut the door behind me. I stared at my reflection before I brushed my teeth and washed my face. I was starting some shower water when the door opened. I spun around as Drake entered. He looked me up and down slowly and licked his lips.

"What are you doing?"

He approached me and stared down at me. He reached behind my legs and lifted me swiftly. I wrapped my legs around his waist and my arms his neck, and he kissed my neck softly. I bit down on my bottom lip as Drake sat me down on the counter.

He released his dick as I slid my panties down. Drake snatched them all the way off and opened my legs. He wrapped his right hand around my neck and gripped my waist firmly with his left. I grabbed his dick, led him to my opening, and guided him inside. The girth made me whimper a little, making him kiss me hard in my mouth.

He stroked me slowly with just the head of his dick, telling me to relax in a near whisper. I widened the gap in between my thighs, and he pulled me further to the edge of the counter. He filled me up even more and even though it hurt a little, I took it. We shared a sloppy tongue kiss as he fucked me harder. He let go of my waist and wrapped both hands around my neck tightly.

I hung my head back and closed my eyes. "Yes..."

Drake kissed my lips. He let my neck go and picked me up off the counter. I wrapped my arms around his neck as he fucked me deeply.

"Drake!" I called out. "Fuck..." I whimpered.

He gripped both of my ass cheeks, guiding me rhythmically up and down his shaft. I had never felt no shit like this. I wanted to moan, cry, curse, and beg. He drilled me harder, whispering in my ear how good my pussy was. Drake then licked my earlobe and swore on his life he wasn't sharing me.

Right after I was cuming. He slammed my back against the bathroom door and fucked me deeper.

I moaned louder. "Baby..."

"I'm right here." He pounded my insides. After a few seconds his body stiffened, and he groaned into my neck.

I held onto him tight as I came down from my orgasm. When he was finished with his, Drake looked me in my eyes before we shared a deep kiss.

ROME

Surprisingly, I was up and full of energy. I let Royal out around midnight and went right back to sleep. After dressing in skinny jeans, an orange Nike hoodie, jean jacket, and white, furry Uggs, I headed out. It was ten-thirty in the morning, but I was wide awake.

I texted my brother Romans' girlfriend, Ava, and she was up too. She said she was at a donut shop and after texting back and forth for a while, we agreed to meet up. When I pulled my white 2019 Genesis G70 Tonio gifted me into the parking lot, Ava was getting out of her matte pink Wraith. I hopped out and when I noticed it was snowing a little, I rolled my eyes. I hated driving in bad weather.

"Hey Rome." Ava smiled as she shut her door.

I adjusted my MK bag on my shoulder. "What's up."

"I hope it doesn't start snowing hard." She opened the door and I followed her inside.

"Right." The smell of freshly baked donuts, and coffee brewing, made my stomach rumble.

Chance stood behind the counter with an apron on and huge smile on her face. "Good morning."

"Good morning."

"What can I get you ladies?" A song by 6lack was playing lowly as she straightened up donuts behind the glass.

Ava found a seat at the counter, right in front of the register. "Let me get a coffee. I've been trying to wake up for two hours, yo." She placed her purse in the seat next to her. "I was up with Roman's horny ass all night."

I gagged a little. The last thing I wanted to envision was Tonio or Twin getting it in.

Ew.

"Coming right up." Chance laughed. "What you want Rome? It's on the house." She began making Ava's coffee.

"Let me get a caramel frappe and a glazed donut." I sat in the seat next to Ava's purse.

"What did you do yesterday?" Ava removed a MacBook out of her purse. "What True end up getting you?"

"Girl, tickets to see Ella Mai in Cali on Sunday. Erin said she'll stay out there and go with me."

"That sounds like fun." Ava replied, more focused on whatever was on her computer screen. "I wanna go."

"I got an extra ticket." Chance slid her coffee in front of her. "I made True promise that if I couldn't find nobody to give it to, he had to come with me."

Ava shook her head.

Chance started on my frappe. "What did you and Ro end up doing?" She giggled. "Besides screw."

I snickered. Ava and Roman would be in the middle of arguing and then they'd end up in the bathroom. It didn't matter where they were.

"We went to a Valentine's Day party at Rajon's school and then went home and chilled." She shrugged. "He said he has a surprise for me today."

Chance placed the frappe in front of me. She put a glazed donut in this fancy edible paper. "I know what it is." She beamed handing me my donut and a napkin.

Ava's eyes shot up from her MacBook. "Tell me."

I chuckled taking a bite out of the donut. I thought Lamar's had fire donuts; they didn't have shit on Chance's.

"If I tell you, then it won't be a surprise. Now will it?"

"Whatever." Ava sipped from her coffee.

"What about you, Rome?" Chance looked to me. "What did you end up doing?"

"Nothing for real." There was no way that I was going to tell them about Royal. Ava and Chance were cool and all, but I didn't know them like that.

Chance pouted playfully. "You could've dropped by. After True and Drake left, I didn't do nothing but wash clothes."

"Domesticated ass." Ava joked.

Chance rolled her eyes. "Whatever."

I wiped my mouth down with a napkin. "How did y'all choose your career paths?"

Chance leaned forward on the counter. "True pitched the idea to me. The location and everything." She smiled.

"And True is your boyfriend, right?" I'd met True a few times. He was super intimidating and quiet. But I guess what he lacked in personality he made up for in looks. True was fine to the point where you had to do a double take whenever he entered the room. I know I did.

Ava made some kind of noise and Chance shot her a look.

"No, True's my best friend. Nothing more, nothing less."

I nodded. "What you about you?" I asked Ava.

"Kai Money saw I was book smart and paid for me to go to business school. Everything else just kind of fell into place." She shrugged.

I looked down at my frappe. "Tonio wants me to go to school."

"You don't want to?" Chance asked as people started entering her shop.

"Rome come to talk to me." Ava got down from her seat and I followed her to a table near the window. "I've been trying to find an assistant I can trust. I have one back in New York, her name is Zahara."

I glanced out of the window as large snowflakes fell from the sky, then back to her.

"I'm running my two shops, I handle everything on the business end for my brothers' and their women, and last summer Tone made me his business partner."

Damn.

Since I had known Ava, I'd gotten this feeling that she was a boss bitch. She was always dressed fly, drove crazy whips, and she stayed giving orders on the phone. A few times out of the week she would come to the Morris Mansion and meet with Tonio in his office. Twin said she had a bad attitude, but I hadn't seen that side of her. But then again, she worked with Tonio, so I knew she was with the shits.

"I'm looking for help and if you're down, you can start Monday." She stared at me. "Just know I don't tolerate laziness, and you can't bullshit a bullshitter." Ava sipped from her mug.

I nodded.

"I'll give you until Sunday to give me an answer." She opened her MacBook.

DRAKE

"I guess I'll see you later."

"A'ight." I unlocked the doors.

Brela: *Why haven't I heard from you.*

Me: *Busy*

Erica sucked her teeth, making me look over at her. After a quiet ride home, we made it back to Kansas City. I knew she had an attitude, but I didn't care. I just wanted her little ass to get out my whip. I had shit I needed to do.

Her body language told me she was in the mood to argue. I couldn't right now, I had to get to the city. I had been gone longer than I anticipated. Roman was waiting on me so we could roll up on a couple suckas. I would get with her spoiled ass later.

Brela: *Stop by and see me. I want some dick.*

I shook my head. Brela was an older chick I'd been fuckin' since I got out the pen two months ago. She cooked meals, washed my clothes, and stayed tryna clock a niggas every move like I was her nigga. Brela was ten years older than me and gave the best top. Shit between us wasn't serious, but Brela was most def in my fab five.

Me: *Get wit you later*

"Are you really texting a bitch like I'm not right here?" Erica pushed her door open.

I shook my head. "The fuck is your problem?" Her ass had been acting funny since I dicked her down earlier.

"You stupid ass niggas is my problem." She shot back and hopped out.

"Don't forget your bag." I reminded her, tossing my head towards the backseat.

Erica slammed the passenger door and opened the back. Once she had her belongings, she slammed that door hard too.

I rolled down the passenger window. "You break it, you buy it." I chuckled at her mad ass.

She flipped me off with her back to me as she headed inside.

~

"Wassup wit' you." Roman hopped in the car, shut the door, and gave me dap.

I pulled away from the curb. "Shit, I can't call it."

He sparked up a blunt. "I hope this shit don't take all day. I still need to get shit together for Ava's shop." Roman was surprising Ava with a tattoo shop. She already had two in New York, but he said she was always complaining about how much she missed them.

The snow picked up.

"These lil' niggas better not play wit' me today." He passed me the L to me.

"On God."

Twenty minutes later we pulled up in the hood. Even though it was cold and snowing, the block was still hot. I put my whip in park and me Ro finished off the rest of the blunt. My eyes skimmed the block and when I saw Royal pull up, I smirked knowing shit was about to get ugly. Roman rolled his window down.

"Yo, Royal!" He called out.

Royal made his way over to the whip, giving a few of the homies pound. He leaned in the window and Roman handed him the blunt he had just sparked up.

"What y'all niggas got up?"

"Shit." Roman leaned back in his seat.

"There go that nigga right there." I tossed my chin up.

Kadeem got out his jeep. His punk ass was a thief. The stash house he worked at kept coming up short. It was one of the main spots for our cash and dope. Roman was the first one to notice shit was out of whack because Ava brought it to his attention.

Tone didn't even know yet. And since we were about to handle it, he didn't need to. My cuzzo was already taking over in major ways for the Dons. So, naturally we felt obligated to keep shit on the home front under control. He'd always been his brothers' keeper, now it was our turn to be his.

"Aye, Kadeem!" Royal called out. He passed the weed back into the car.

Kadeem tossed his head up. "'Sup, Royal." He stared at my car for a minute.

"I bet that nigga take off running." Roman puffed the blunt coolly.

"I ain't got the energy today." I turned 21 Savage's "4L" down. Erica's pussy drained a nigga something serious. I came so much I wanted to take a nap, but knew I had to get back home.

Kadeem started backtracking to his whip and I popped my locks.

"Told ya..." Roman put the blunt in the ashtray.

Royal got in the backseat just as Kadeem hopped into his jeep and peeled off.

I smacked my lips. "Bitch ass..." I sped off after him and Roman reached down onto the floor and picked up his AR. My Glock was already sitting in my lap.

Royal let his window down and started bussin' first. It probably wasn't a good idea to have a rolling shootout, in the middle of day, while it was snowing, but aye...

ROYAL

While Drake chased Kadeem down, I dumped on his truck. His punk ass was speeding down residential streets. I wasn't trying to hit no innocent bystander, so I couldn't really get down like I wanted to. When he turned a couple corners I knew he was leading us to his homies on the block he was raised on. I removed my clip, flipped it over, and put it back in.

The passenger in Kadeem's jeep started shooting back. Roman hung half-way out of the window and started spraying; causing Kadeem to swerve and jump the curb. He crashed into a tree, and Drake came to a crazy stop a few feet away. We hopped out of the G-Wagon simultaneously. Kadeem jumped out of his car with his gun pointed and Drake sent a bullet through his dome. The passenger hopped out blasting, and then took off running. I emptied the rest of my clip into his back and he fell forward.

We rushed back to Drake's whip as the sounds of police sirens got near. Just as I was about to shut my door, I bullet whizzed by me. The second hit me right in the shoulder, the third nicked the side of my head. I dropped down into the floor of the backseat.

"Aye, pass me a banger."

Drake tossed his glock to me.

As he sped off I got up. I hung out of the window lettin' off on a group of niggas. They were Kadeem's homies. I dropped two and then fell back into the car. Police sirens got closer as Drake zoomed through the streets.

"You good?" Roman asked me over his shoulder.

"I'm straight. Got hit up twice, though." My adrenaline was still going so the pain hadn't hit me yet.

"We gon' drop you off wit' Doc." Roman sparked the blunt up, took a puff and handed it to me.

8
NEVER PANIC...
ERICA

Two days later...

Loud talking could be heard in the kitchen as I neared. When I cut the corner, my eyes immediately landed on Drake. He glanced up at me, smirked, and then looked back down at his phone. Tone, who was leaning against the counter eating hot fries, was talking to Roman. I made my way to the refrigerator.

"Wassup, Erica." Lucus spoke. "You can't speak?"

I grabbed a water. "Hey..." I replied dryly, unscrewing the cap.

"What you bouta get into?"

My eyes rolled to Drake and he was staring at me. My gaze then shifted back to Lucus. "Why?"

"Just asking." He licked his lips.

I rolled my eyes.

"I see you comin' through drippin' and shit."

Absentmindedly I looked down at my wrist. I was wearing both the tennis bracelet, and Rollie.

"That lil' nigga finally bossed up I see."

My eyes shot back to Drake. "Yeah. My nigga loves me." I started back out of the kitchen.

"That nigga don't give a fuck about you."

I stopped in my tracks and spun around. All eyes, except for Tones, were on Drake. Lucus laughed, but it stopped just as soon as he started when Drake looked at him.

"I don't know why you lookin' all hurt for." Drake chuckled. "You already knew that."

"Fuck you."

"Again?"

My eyes grew at how bold his ass was. Why the fuck would he say that? Tone and Roman acted like they weren't phased, but I knew soon everybody would know we had sex.

"You smashin' shorty?" Lucus cheesed back and forth between us. "My nigga..." He said proudly.

Embarrassed, I stormed out of the kitchen.

"Erica!" Drake called after me.

I ignored him.

"You don't hear me?" His tone hardened.

I faced him. "What?"

His eyebrows furrowed. "Lower your voice."

I smacked my lips. "You just embarrassed me."

His eyes danced around me in confusion. "Embarrassed? How?"

With my free hand, I pointed towards the kitchen. "You just basically told everyone we were fuckin'. Now they're going to be looking at me all funny." I didn't like the enthusiasm Lucus showed. Had they been talking about me? Betting on who would conquer the pussy first?

Drake waved me off. "Ain't nobody lookin' at your paranoid ass differently. Everybody in that kitchen is fuckin' *somebody*. We all grown." He shrugged. "You grown too, though, right? Ain't that what you told your moms?"

I stared at him defiantly. Why did he have to be so cute? Since my brother was considered a 'thug,' I usually wasn't attracted to that type.

I saw the way Eli treated girls, how he got what he wanted from them and then acted like they didn't exist. But Tate showed me it didn't matter how old, or what background they came from, a nigga was gon' be a nigga. Period.

"Where have you been?" I'd called him several times since the day he dropped me off. Each time he ignored me. Between him and Tate I felt so played.

He inched towards me. "Shit been hectic."

"Too hectic to text me back?" I now had a full-blown attitude.

He shrugged.

"Okay." I spun back around.

"Come take a ride wit' me." I stopped again, and he walked past me.

I stared at the back of his head as he swaggered down the hallway. "I don't feel like going nowhere."

"It wasn't up for debate, and I didn't ask you how you felt."

∽

"I thought I was gon' have to come get you." Drake didn't even let me get in the car all the way.

"I had to put my lashes on." I pulled my seatbelt across my body as he drove away from the house.

He only shook his head. "What you been up to?"

I pulled up my Snapchat. "Looking for a job."

"For what?" Drake removed his gun from his side and sat it in his lap. "You should be focusing on school."

"That was part of the agreement. Erin told me I could move in if I worked a part-time job since I don't do any extra-curricular."

"Then play a sport or something? Join a club."

I frowned. "Like what? It's almost the end of the school year. Plus, my nail tech is already booked two weeks out. What if I break a nail? It might take her a couple days to get me in for a repair." I shook my head. "I'll pass."

Drake chuckled. "Type of shit is that, kid?" He tossed his head up to the security, and they opened the gate.

I shrugged.

"So, you that type of chick." He looked over at me.

"What?" I asked still sifting through filters.

"Spoiled and materialistic."

I decided on the one with bunny ears. "If that's what box you wanna put me in. I'm also an A-B student. It's not my fault I'm cute and my brother and my sister look out for me."

I was tired of people judging my exterior. Just because I liked nice things didn't mean I was an airhead. I appreciated the value of a dollar. I knew most people my age didn't have half the shit or opportunities that I did. I was grateful for everything God blessed me with.

Drake sped down the road. "What you gettin' snappy for?"

Because I was sick of muthafuckas thinking they knew me when they didn't. "I'm not." I focused back on my Snapchat.

He turned the music up.

"Where are we going anyway?" I snapped a picture.

"I need to go home and change first. While I'm doing that you can look up something for us to get into." He frowned at his phone.

I laughed. "How you gon' tell me to come on, but not have anywhere for us to go?"

"I just wanted you with me." Drake stated nonchalantly, texting.

I smiled as I recorded a video of us.

ROME

"Does that hurt?"

"Nah." Royal replied with his eyes closed. His head was in my lap as I cleaned the wound on his head.

"Tell me if I'm being too rough."

He nodded.

We were chilling at his townhouse. For the past two days, I'd come by and keep him company. Not only did a bullet graze the side of his head, but one was stuck in his shoulder. Royal didn't seem phased, though. The only thing that changed was us having to be extra careful during sex. He was still sore, and no matter how tough Royal seemed, he'd wince a few times in pain.

"I still can't believe you got shot and didn't go to the hospital." I put the cleaning supplies in a plastic bag. "What if they don't heal correctly?"

"They will." He kept his eyes closed. "This ain't my first time being shot."

I stared down at him. "Really?"

Royal nodded. "I got hit in my back when I was eleven and last year a nigga tried to take my leg off with a chop." He chuckled.

I scowled at him. I didn't find shit funny. "Is that why you dip a little when you walk?"

Again, he nodded.

"Wow. And you still do the same shit?"

Royal opened his eyes. "The fuck are you talkin' about?"

"You could've died on four different occasions. But you still keep running back to the streets." I considered Royal smart, so him being dumb enough to willingly risk his life didn't sit well with me. "What about Misa?"

"What about her?"

"If something happens to you, she would be devastated."

"Misa is straight. Everything I do is for her. You think I'ma street nigga just for fun? I'm giving Misa what I never had. And even when I'm dead and gone, my baby is gon' be straight."

I frowned. Royal dead? The thought alone had me feeling emotional. He was only twenty-three. There were people his age just finishing college, getting ready to jump into the real world. And here he was working for a crime lord, gambling with his life every day.

"What if that bullet would've done more than nicked you?"

"Then we wouldn't be sitting here. Now would we?"

How could he be so composed? Two days ago, he almost died.

"I guess." I mumbled, giving 'Black Ink Crew' my attention.

"What's the story behind that rose?"

I looked down, and he was looking up at me.

"Huh?"

Royal grabbed the blunt from behind his ear. "The rose. Why put it right there?"

I subconsciously ran my hand across the front of my neck. "I got it to cover up a scar." My eyes rolled back to the television.

Royal lit the blunt. "What happened?"

"When I lived in a group home, a bunch of chicks held me down and wrapped a jump around my neck." I gladly took the blunt from him and took a long puff.

"What the fuck they do that for?"

I exhaled from my nostrils. "I don't wanna talk about it."

He nodded. "When you ready, I'm all ears."

"Thanks." I took a few more hits. "Royal."

"Wassup." He took the blunt from me.

"Is Myka pregnant?"

He paused to hit the weed.

As I waited on his answer, I flipped through channels.

"She was."

I looked down at him again. "Was as in? She lost it? Took a plan B? Got an abortion?"

"We took care of it."

"So, you're still fuckin' her?"

"I was."

"And when did you stop?"

Royal shrugged. "It's been a minute.

"Mmmm..."

"What's that for?"

Cause I don't believe you.

"Royal, I'm not into all that fighting and arguing. I told you that. If you're still sleeping with her, then maybe I should fall back."

He handed me the blunt.

"I'm already trying to find my way."

"Rome I'm not fuckin' her and she ain't pregnant, Ma."

Deciding to take his word, I relaxed back into my seat. The TV was now showing 'Ridiculousness'. We watched the showing laughing, both high as hell. When we got the munchies, I got up, and warmed up our food from 'Fuzzy's Taco'. I stopped and got us both cheesy potato burritos, with chips and Queso.

My phone sounded off just as I laid our food out on the table. Erica's name flashed across the screen.

"Hello?" I sat down.

"Ro Ro, what you doing?"

"Eating."

"Are you with Royal?"

I looked over at him. He was already tearing through his food without saying Grace. I rolled my eyes.

"Yeah, why?"

"Y'all should come to the Escape room with me and Drake."

"Drake?" I frowned. "Drake Morris? My cousin?"

"Yep." She chirped. "Please come. The more people it is the more fun it will be."

"Erica, when did you and Dra—"

"We'll talk when I see you." She cut me off. "So, you're coming, right?"

"Hold on." I muted the phone. "Erica wants to go to the escape room."

"Okay?" He stuffed his face. "Go head. I'm probably about to turn a couple corners anyway."

"She invited us both. It's a double date."

Royal shook his head no.

"Why not?"

"'Cause I don't fuck wit' niggas."

"It's Drake."

He smirked, shaking his head. "That nigga..."

I couldn't believe it either. Little spoiled, naive Erica, with ruthless, jail bird Drake. Who would've thought?

I unmuted the phone. "Erica?"

"I'm still here."

"Text me the time and place."

DRAKE

When I got out the shower, Erica was laying across my bed. I dropped my towel, approached the bed, and pulled her to the edge by her ankle. She looked off bashfully when I stood between her legs and hovered over her. Erica looking real fly in some skin tight, cut up jeans, a white body suit, and glitter Uggs that matched her purse.

Her hair was parted down the middle, tucked behind her ears, draping down her back. She smelled good too. She gazed up at me while biting down on her bottom lip. With my hands planted on both sides of her head, I leaned down and kissed her. Erica grabbed my face and kissed me back, slipping her tongue into my mouth.

Ding, dong.

I pulled away.

Ding, dong

My doorbell went off again.

"Who is that?" Erica sat up on her elbows.

"I don't know." I frowned, standing up straight.

Nobody came to the crib unannounced.

Ding, dong

I went to my dresser, removed a pair of sweats, and put 'em on. I grabbed my burner and exited the room.

Ding, dong

When I approached the door, I looked through the peephole.

The fuck...

I smacked my lips.

"This bitch trippin'." I unlocked the door and pulled it open. "Wassup."

"Hey." Brela smiled. "I brought Chinese takeout." She held the bag up. Brela knew Chinese was my shit.

"Why you ain't call first?" I stared down at her.

She shrugged. "I figured you would be here. I know you usually come home, shower, and relax for a few hours."

I looked back inside my condo. "I got company right now."

Brela's face dropped. "Really, Drake." She sucked her teeth.

I shrugged.

"I just saw you this morning."

By 'saw', she meant 'fucked'.

Again, I shrugged.

"Drake, who's at the door?" Erica came up behind me.

Brela smiled. "I live in the building. I was dropping by to thank him for giving my car a jump the other day." She looked up at me.

"No problem." I gave her a slight nod.

"I better get going before my food gets cold." Brela's smile widened. "Thanks again." And with that she took off down the hall.

∼

After I smoked a blunt and got dressed, we headed out. Erica wanted to do some shit called 'Escape Room'. Since I said it was her pick, I was down to try it out. We pulled up the same time Royal and Rome did. Erica of course was playing in her phone, making a video and shit.

Her phone went off and she smacked her lips before answering. "Hello?"

I turned off the car.

"Tate you know why I'm ignoring you."

I looked over at her. She shook her head, looked out of her window, and then sighed.

"'Cause you been acting funny lately. Nothing with us is the same. You only call me when you see I'm not blowing you up."

"Erica, stop playin' with' me, man." I opened my door.

Her neck snapped in my direction. "What?"

I got out the whip as Rome approached the passenger side.

"Hey cousin." She smiled.

"Wassup cuzzo. Yo brothers know you here?" Royal was my nigga and all, but Rome was blood.

She shrugged and opened Erica's door.

"Tate, bye. I don't feel like arguing with you."

"Nah, you don't feel like getting fucked up." I corrected her.

She cut her eyes at me and Rome laughed, shaking her head.

"What's good, foo?"

"I can't call it." I slapped fives with Royal after I shut my door.

Erica got out of the car, still on the phone, arguing. I walked around the front of my G-wagon to her. Snatching her phone out of her hand, I looked down on her.

"Drake!" she screwed her face up.

"Why you bein' disrespectful?"

"Give me my phone."

I headed for the building.

"Drake, give me my phone."

When we stepped inside, Erica was still whining about her phone. I tuned her out as me and Royal picked which Escapes we wanted to do, and then paid.

"Drake." Erica leaned on the counter. "Can I please have my phone back?" She looked cute when she was pouting.

I shook my head no.

"I wanna Snapchat this."

"She just said you can't bring phones in."

"Okay, you guys can follow me." The lady came from behind the counter.

I grabbed Erica by her forearm before she took off. "Don't ever answer the phone for another nigga when you're with me."

She rolled her eyes. "He kept callin'."

"So?"

Erica raised her hand in a mock surrender and stepped around me. "Okay, Daddy."

I shook my head at her as she rushed to catch up with Rome and hooked arms.

ROYAL

After the Escape Room, I dropped Rome off at the compound. She had me drop her off at Sadee's. I was done trying to figure out why she was scared for Tone to know about us. She was his baby sister, but she wasn't a baby. Rome was advanced for her age.

"Call from Myka..." came from the speakers. I answered the phone and lit the blunt in my hand.

"Yeah?"

"Well, hello to you too."

I switched lanes.

"Misa wants to talk to you."

"A'ight."

Myka smacked her lips. "Here."

"Daddy what you doing?" Misa's soft voice seeped through the speakers.

"Driving. What you doin'?"

"Nothing." She sighed. "Daddy, I lost my iPad."

I shook my head. "How you do that?"

"I...I...." She paused "I left it on the bus."

"After I told you not to take it out the damn house." Myka snapped in the background. "Her ass is hardheaded."

"Mini me, why you ain't listen to your mama?"

"I wanted to show my friends my dress up game."

"After I told you, you couldn't." Myka instigated.

"Tell yo mama I said shut up." I shook my head.

"Mama my Daddy said, shut up."

"You shut up, and Misa don't play with me."

I chuckled. "Misa, man, you gotta listen to yo mama when she tell you to do something. Now look, somebody got your shit."

"I know." She pouted. "Daddy?"

"Wassup, Mini me?" I blew a cloud of weed from my nostrils.

"Can you buy me another one?"

I pulled up on a stop sign just as my phone started beeping showing a call from Rome.

"Daddy, can you?" Misa asked again. "I won't take it out the house."

"Yeah Mini me, I got you."

"Okay!" She said excitedly. "My mama wanna talk to you."

My phone beeped again.

"You shouldn't even be getting another iPad." Myka started again. "Go brush your teeth for bed." Misa said something back that made Myka smack her lips. "Misa Royale, get the fruit snacks and then go do what I said."

I shook my head. Myka talked the most shit about our daughter being spoiled, but she probably spoiled her the most. Misa's shoe game was sick for a seven-year-old, her braids stayed fresh, and her wardrobe was extensive. Every other week her finger nails were a different color, and she was already asking to carry a purse. Myka was just in her feelings because she probably had a fucked up day.

"Royal..."

"Wassup?"

"I heard about you getting shot. Why didn't you call me? Misa heard it from your sister's friend when she was over there. Luna had to lie and cover it up."

"It wasn't shit."

She sucked her teeth. "You need to be more careful. Misa needs you here."

"I know."

"And the new baby does too." She slipped that last part in, in a mumble.

"New baby?" I frowned. When she didn't respond, I clenched my jaws. "Myka..."

"I'm keeping the baby, Royal."

Man...

"I know you don't want me to, but I am. We don't have to be together, but it's my body. My choice." Myka snapped. "You should've strapped up if me being your baby mama is so horrible."

I put the weed doobie in the ashtray.

"I already told your parents and Misa knows too."

I rubbed my hand up and down the back of my neck. "Myka, why you makin' shit harder than it need to be?"

"Royal, bye." She banged on me.

"Man..." I drawled loudly. I wanted to it put my foot up Myka's ass. The only reason I wasn't going to was because I took full responsibility. I called Rome, still rubbing the back of my neck. It was something I did to relax, a reminder that what was done was done.

"Hello..."

"What's good, Romie Rome."

"Hey. I start working with Ava tomorrow. She wants me to be there at eight, which means I'll have to be up and out the house a little after seven if I wanna be on time. Plus, I don't know how traffic is going to be."

"Rome, stop rambling and just get to the point, shorty."

"Can I come stay the night? You don't have to pick me up, I can drive myself. And I'll be gone before you wake up in the morning."

"I'm not gone be at the crib until later. I'll call you when I'm on my way." Rome didn't need an excuse to come to the house. She had been looking out for me the past couple days and I actually liked her being there.

"Okay."

"If it gets too late, I'll have you come get the key." I flipped my turn signal. "Matter fact meet me at the house now so I can let you in."

"I'll see you in a minute."

"Okay." She hung up and a text from Myka came through.

Myka: *Dr. appt Friday. Come please*

9

ONE STEP FORWARD, THREE STEPS BACK

ERICA

The lunch bell and I grabbed my backpack. Instead of going to my locker, I made sure I had my car keys and headed for the entrance. After a three-day suspension I shouldn't have been on, I was officially over high school. The one class me and Anais had together was awkward as hell. Rome told me about her trip to Starbucks, I would've paid to see Rome beat her ass with a shoe.

"Erica!"

I spun around only to see Tate walking in my direction. He was with a couple of his boys, and they were all dressed alike, looking corny as hell. I crossed my arms and waited for him to approach me.

"Where you going?"

"Why, Tate?"

He wrapped his arms around my waist and pulled me close. "You really ain't fuckin' with me, huh?"

"At all."

His boys laughed, making him squeeze me.

"I miss you."

"Right." I missed him too, but he didn't need to know that. Yeah Tate had his ways, but he was my first. Call me dumb, but I thought that should've counted for something. But it didn't. Which was why I had been crying myself to sleep every night.

"You don't believe me?" He smiled, showcasing his pearly whites. "Let's go get lunch together."

Before I could object and tell him no, he was telling his boys good bye, and pulling me along.

∼

"What colors you wanna wear to prom?" Tate asked taking a bite out of his sweet and sour chicken.

I frowned, mixing my rice. "I'm not going."

"Why come?"

I grabbed a napkin. "Tate, why are you acting like we're together still?"

"When did we break up?"

I looked at him like he was crazy. He had to be. "When you stood me up on Valentine's Day, *after* you promised you were going to do something special."

"I thought we were past that." He continued scarfing down his food. "Let's not act like you ain't been flexing." He stopped eating to side eye me.

"Me? Flexing?" I knew he was talking about my videos with Drake. He commented on each one he saw, talking shit. We were the hottest topic at school right now.

"Who is he?"

"A friend." I shrugged.

"Well, you can dead that." He stuffed his mouth. "Nigga look like he been in prison his whole life." Tate snorted.

I rolled my eyes. "Tate, I don't wanna be with you anymore. I don't even know why I let you talk me into coming here." I pushed my chair back. "I'm out."

Tate grabbed my wrist tightly. "Sit the fuck down, Erica."

I tried to snatch away from him, and his grip tightened. "Tate, let my arm go."

He looked around the restaurant and then pushed my hand away. I grabbed my purse. "Lose my fuckin' number."

He got up from the table. "Sit down."

"Or what?" I mugged him.

Tate snatched my purse from me, unzipped it and emptied everything out of it.

"What the fuck is wrong with you!" I screamed pushing him. Tate was completely out of character. We argued a lot, but he never tripped like this.

He pushed me back and I stumbled a little.

"Excuse me, you can't do that in here." The hostess neared our table.

"Erica, I'm sorry." Tate started helping me pick the contents of my purse up.

I ignored him.

"I'm just going through a lot right now, baby. School and ball are stressing a nigga out."

Tears blurred my vision. Not because I was sad, though. I was pissed the fuck off. I just wanted Tate to stop talking to me and let me go in peace. I didn't care about his apology or excuses. I needed to get away from him before I blacked out on his ass.

Once I had all my belongings back in my purse, I grabbed my parka from the back of my chair.

"Erica." Tate put some cash on the table.

I slipped my arms into my jacket as I made my way out of the restaurant.

"Erica!" Tate rushed after me. "Wait, man, damn."

The first tear dropped and slipped down my cheek. "Leave me alone, Tate!" When I got to my car, he grabbed my arm.

"Erica. I said I was sorry." Tate's voice softened. "I didn't mean to make you cry."

I wiped my face.

"Stop crying." He pulled me into a hug. "I was tripping. You know I love you."

Do you?

I didn't think Tate ever loved me.

"Let's go to my house and talk." He rocked me from side to side. "Let me make it up to you."

I sucked my teeth and pulled away from him. "I'm going back to school." One thing I didn't do was skip for some dick.

Tate nodded. "Can we talk later on? My sister is out of town for a few days so it'll just be us."

I unlocked my doors. "Tate, fuck you." I opened the door and tossed my purse into the passenger seat.

"It's like that?"

I got inside. "Just like that." I slammed my door, started my car, and pulled out of the parking spot.

ROME

I had been up since seven and it was now going on one in the afternoon. For Valentine's Day, Twin gifted Ava a space for her tattoo shop. It was two levels, with a dope ass brass, spiral staircase right in the middle of the floorplan. The second floor had a balcony that overlooked the lower level. I couldn't wait to see the final outcome once she decorated.

"Tomorrow we can go look at furniture." Ava swiped on her iPad.

I nodded. Ava wanted to do modern designs. She said she wanted the shop 'ratchet classy'. I laughed when she said that, but her ass was dead serious.

"Roman just texted and said he's bringing Chinese. You want something?"

I closed the MacBook Air Ava gifted me. "Yeah. I was just about to ask you if you wanted me to get something." I yawned. "Tell him I want orange chicken and spicy lo mein."

She put her phone to her ear.

"Ava, you grew up in the system, right?" I leaned forward on her desk. This room was the only one fully decorated. Twin had Erin and Chance hook her office up. Ava loved the yellow, powder blue, and silver theme. She kept gushing about how Roman paid close attention to her and the things she liked.

She nodded in my direction and then spoke into the phone. "Baby..." She cheesed. "Nothing, chillin' with Rome." Ava shook her head and blushed. "Really? You nasty, yo."

Smiling, I shook my head. I loved love. Ava and Erin wore the shit so well. They were always glowing and laughing. I hoped I found somebody like Tonio or Twin. Someone whose only priority was my happiness.

"Yeah, she wants orange chicken and spicy lo mein." She looked to me. "He's stopping at the gas station, you want something to drink?"

"A red bull."

"Red bull, baby." Ava paused. "I got bottled water in the mini fridge. Okay, bye. Love you too." She hung up and sat her phone down on her glass desk.

"Did growing up without a family fuck up your trust?" I got more comfortable in the chair, pulled my legs up, and crossed them in my lap.

Ava shrugged. "I guess. Why you ask that?"

Because Royal was doing all the right things, but I knew that shit was just a cover up. I was waiting on his true colors to show at any moment. People always treated you nice before they fucked you over.

"I've been seeing Royal." Just like Erin, Ava was cool and down to Earth. Ava was a little more extreme than E, but they were both genuine people.

Ava smirked. "Oh yeah?"

I nodded. "His baby mama and him have this weird ass relationship, though."

She scoffed. "Do they live together?"

"No."

"Well that's a good start. When I first started fuckin' with Roman, he was living with Leah."

I frowned. "And you let that go down?" I refused to believe Ava Lane let that slide.

"Hell no. But just because he moved out didn't mean the drama stopped. Between Leah and your mom, a bitch couldn't catch a break." Ava pointed to her purse. "But I keep a taser so it's whatever."

I laughed.

"No, but for real, when you say *weird*, what do you mean?"

"Her and her friends play on my phone all day, and even went so far as to try and add me on social media. Royal says they don't fuck with each other like that. But I don't know." If I opened up completely to Royal and he played me... I frowned just thinking about it.

"Does he try to hide you from her?"

I shook my head no.

"Does he disrespect you for her?"

Once again, I shook my head no.

"Does he let it be known that he fuck wit' you the long way?"

I nodded yes.

On Valentine's, I guess Myka called my phone and Royal picked up. The next day she sent this long ass text message about how I could have him. She was bothered as fuck because she started going off on me too and I didn't even do shit. I read the messages she sent and then deleted them. Myka's beef was with Royal, not me.

"Then in the words of the wise Blaze Santiago, 'until he gives you a reason, don't count him out'." She shrugged.

"Blaze Santiago?"

"My sister. She's married to my brother Kai."

I nodded.

"I'm guessing Tone nor Roman knows."

"Nope."

"Why not?" She smirked.

I chuckled. "Have you seen my brothers?" Tonio and Twin weren't friendly ... at all. They were only nice to the women and kids in our family. Anybody else they could give a fuck about. Permanent mean mugs, anger problems, and pure crazy, were the makings of my siblings.

Ava laughed. "Roman might be cooler about it then Tone." She was probably right about that. "But you're grown Rome. And at the end of the day, it doesn't matter that you've just met your brothers, they love yo ass to death. There's nothing you could do to change that."

I needed to hear that. When I first moved to Kansas City, I felt like an outcast. No one ever treated me like one, but people always put up fronts. The relationships I was building with my brothers was slowly but surely progressing. Tonio gave me whatever I wanted, and Twin dropped money off to me every other day while making small conversation.

Ava got up from her seat. "Don't forget to set up the meeting with the caterers for the grand opening. I want finger foods ... nothing messy."

I guess that was Ava's way of saying break over. I grabbed my MacBook, getting right back to work. I was learning fast that she always had something for me to do. I wasn't complaining, though. The pay was good, and I had the opportunity to soak up free game and knowledge. I listened intently as she continued giving off orders.

DRAKE

I leaned back in the seat, still lowkey aggravated. Had been for about thirty minutes now. Seeing Erica hugged up with that lil' bum, had a real nigga bothered. Roman hopped out the whip the same time she hopped in hers. I didn't even have an appetite after seeing that shit.

Crazy, right?

Roman thought the shit was funny. That's why I had him drop me off to my car. I knew Erica got out of school at quarter to three. Which gave me enough time to take care of a money situation and hit a few spots up. After I was done, I pulled up to her school, and parked in front her car so she couldn't get out of her parking spot.

When she came out and saw my car, she looked confused. I hopped out my whip and met her half way.

"What are you doing here?"

I grabbed her bookbag from her. "I ain't talked to you since yesterday morning." We walked side by side.

"I know, I had to catch up with school." Erica wrapped her arm around mine. "I slacked off and fell behind."

I nodded.

"So, you came all the way here to see me." She snickered. "Because you haven't talked to me?"

I shrugged.

"You're a bad liar." Erica giggled.

I frowned. "What?" We stopped walking.

Erica looked up at me, smiling. Licking my lips, I grabbed the collar of her Nike hoodie. She smirked. "You were with Roman." She smiled harder. "I saw him as I was pulling off."

I smacked my lips.

"That's the only reason you're here right now." Erica pulled away from me. "Jealous much?" She took off walking.

Me? Jealous? Nah...

"You back fuckin' wit' that clown?"

"And if I am?" She stopped again and asked smartly.

I eyed her pretty little ass. "Are you?"

Erica rolled her eyes. "No. That was a farewell lunch date."

"Erica, can we talk?" A chick walked up on us. She looked up at me in wonderment.

"No, Anais." Erica's tone was flat. "I don't feel like talking to you."

"I was only trying to have your back since you swear I don't." Ole girl snapped back. "Tate is going around showing his boys your nudes and videos of you sucking his dick." She spun back around and walked off.

Erica took of back to the entrance and I grabbed her by her purse.

"Where you going?"

"To whoop Tate's ass!" She yelled, and her voice cracked. "I'm so fuckin' tired of him."

"Nah, you getting your ass in the car and going home." I spoke firmly. Erica didn't need to be getting suspended, missing school again over that bitch nigga. "Go home and chill out." I pulled her toward me.

Erica huffed and then wiped the tears from her face. "I swear to God I hate his ass." She snatched away from me. "Give me my bag." She snatched that too and stormed away.

I followed her.

"Move your car!"

"What you mad at me for?" I frowned. "I didn't do shit to you." We got to her car and she opened her back door to throw her bag inside. I opened the driver's door for her. "You spazzing out on the wrong muthafucka, kid."

Erica got behind the wheel without a word.

I held onto her door while she pouted.

"I'ma fuck him up." She punched the steering wheel.

"Just do what I said, a'ight?"

She started the ignition and then pulled her seatbelt across her body. "Can you shut my door, so I can go?"

I took a step back and closed the door. I hopped in my ride and peeled out of the parking lot.

∼

"You sure this the spot?" I passed the blunt to Lucus but spoke to his little sister Raven who was sitting in the backseat behind him.

"Yep. I was over here for a kickback last week." She spoke. "And he was just on Snapchat like twenty minutes ago."

"And that Kiara chick is here?" I looked through my side mirror and then scanned the block.

"Yeah, her and Tate." Raven took the blunt from Lucus.

"I been wanting that bitches head for the longest." My other little cousin, and their sister Aspen said. "Dick riding ass bitch." She tried to open her door and get out, but it was locked.

"Aye..." I frowned. "Hol' up. Rowdy ass lil' nigga."

Aspen just like her brother and sister was my Aunt Daisy's kid. She was junior at Central High School. Her and Raven were wild on behalf of their moms *and* pops being drunks. They were eighteen and sixteen years old, and both had babies of their own. My moms used to always have a story to tell me about them when I was locked up.

"Nah, Raven wouldn't let me drag her ass last time I saw her."

"Girl, because you had one hand in a cast." Raven snapped. "The fuck was you gon' do with one hand?"

"Bitch I got two feet."

I shook my head. "Shut up."

The car went silent.

"Raven call 'em."

A few seconds went by and then... "Tate. Wassup this is Raven. Yeah, I'm outside." She paused. "Okay."

Tate was a petty hustler. Lil' nigga was selling weed to high schoolers. I'm guessing he was making a little money for a kid his age, 'cause Raven pointed his matte green Jeep out to me. The front door to the house he was in opened. Tate stepped out, looked around, and then headed for my Charger. I unlocked the doors and Raven hopped out.

"Hey, Tate."

"Wassup Raven, baby."

I opened my door and got out and Lucus followed suit.

"What the fuck?" I heard the panic in Tate's voice.

Lucus's fist sent Tate stumbling backwards. Tate recovered from the punch and threw a lick back but missed. Lucus three pieced his bitch ass and he fell.

"Whoop his ass brother!" Aspen yelled.

The front door to the house opened again and the chick from earlier stepped out. Her scary ass went right back in the inside. But not too long after she did another chick came running out.

"Get the fuck off of him!" She ran up and stole off on Lucus.

I blinked, and Raven and Aspen were on her ass. I stood on the side line watching Lucus stomp out Tate, and the girls drag Kiara. I grabbed the blunt from behind my ear and removed the lighter from my pocket. After sparking the blunt and hitting it a few times, I cleared my throat.

"A'ight." I pushed off my whip.

Lucus stepped back, Raven let go of Kiara, but Aspen wouldn't let go of her hair. Lucus bear hugged her and then picked her up. Tate coughed and whimpered as I approached him. I hovered over him and put my blunt out on the middle of his forehead. I wanted to do more than that, but the lil' nigga couldn't even hang with Lucus; the fuck was he gon' do with me?

"If Erica tell me you fuckin' wit' her again, I'ma be back."

I made my way back to the driver's side and got in. Lucus shut his door and let his seat back. Raven hopped in and once Aspen emptied out Tate's pockets she got in last.

"I'ma going shopping tomorrow." She laughed. "Bitch ass nigga."

ROYAL

"Thank you for coming with me."

I nodded as I held the door open for Myka.

"Let's stop and get something to eat." She looked at her Apple Watch. "I took off today and I don't have to get Misa from my dad until five."

"We can stop at Freddy's." I offered since it was close to her Doctors office.

"Okay cool."

When I picked Misa up for school this morning, Myka reminded me she had an appointment. She was indeed pregnant; due in July. I wasn't happy with her decision to keep the baby, but since she was, I accepted it. I wasn't gon' treat this baby no different than I treated my Mini me. They were a product of me and my legacy.

When we got in the car, Myka talked nonstop about what she wanted it to be. She wanted a boy and I wanted another girl. Misa wanted a little sister, so she was outnumbered. We got to Freddy's and after ordering, and making our drinks, we found a free table.

"I'm about to tear this burger up. I didn't eat this morning." She stared down at her phone. "Misa had to have breakfast at school."

"Why?" I glanced around the restaurant.

Myka sipped from her drink. "I woke up late and was having morning sickness." She rolled her eyes. "Dry heaving and shit."

"I would've brought y'all something." I ignored Rome's call.

She shrugged. "I probably wouldn't have kept it down. For some reason I can't eat before twelve."

I nodded.

"So, you with that Rome chick now? Is that who Misa helped you shop for on Valentine's Day?"

I nodded.

Myka chuckled sarcastically. "You are so disrespectful. How the fuck you gon' take *my* child and have her pick out shit for another bitch."

"Watch your mouth."

She sucked her teeth. "Good luck with that. The bitch ain't even all that cute."

I ran my hand down the back of my neck.

"And how old is she? Like twelve?"

"Myka, shut up, man."

Rome: *I wanna have sex. Lol. I got thirty minutes. We can do it in the car*

I chuckled.

"That must be her."

Me: *Can't today Romie Rome*

They called our order out and I went to get it. When I got back to the table, Myka was on the phone.

"Just got back from the Doctors, girl." She grabbed her burger.

Rome: *Ok*

That's why I fucked with Rome. She didn't hassle me all day, whining and complaining about time and attention. Rome didn't give a fuck because she knew I'd see her sooner than later. She was smart and patient enough to understand sometimes I couldn't just drop what I was doing 'cause she wanted me to. She would see me when I got home since she had been spending the night all week.

"Let me call you back when I finish eating."

I started on my food.

"Has Misa met her?"

"Once."

"Royal." She sighed. "Let me have another nigga around Misa, it'll be a different story."

"And?"

Myka shook her head. "I'm not even bouta start with you."

We sat in silence as we ate. After I dropped Myka off I had other shit to do. Tone was out of town and Erin wanted to go to her mom's house. She called and told me she could drive herself, and after checking with Tone he said it was cool. All I had to do was meet her there and then follow her home to make sure she got there safely.

"Are you going to tell her about the baby?"

I didn't want to. But what choice did I have?

"She gon' be cool with that?"

"Let me worry about Rome."

"That's a no." She sipped from her straw. "I hope you don't think you're about to keep my baby a secret. And I'm not about to hide my pregnancy."

I frowned. "I didn't tell you to." Wasn't shit I could do about Myka being pregnant.

"I can't wait to start shopping for little tiny shoes and clothes." She wiped her mouth down.

Luna: *Daddy said call him.*

Me: *Yep*

"We should go and get Misa's new iPad today, so she can stop bothering me about it." She mumbled messing with her phone.

"Call the Apple Store and see if they busy." I finished my food off.

Myka did what I told her, and I went to throw our trash away. After I refilled my drink, we left out. We sat in the parking lot as I rolled up and she talked to the Apple people.

"The one at Town Center isn't busy." She faced me. "You wanna lock in 2:30?"

I nodded, sealing my blunt.

"Two-thirty is fine." She verified.

I sparked my blunt.

Myka hung up and turned the heat up. "Freezing Moo is near there. I can get some ice cream." She secured her seatbelt.

I pulled out of the parking lot and turned my music all the way up.

10

AIN'T NO SUCH THING AS TOO FAST
ERICA

I cried myself to sleep when I got home from school. I didn't want to make the long drive to the compound, so I ended up at my moms. I was happy she wasn't home, because I ugly cried for about thirty minutes. I was finding out the hard way that fucking with Tate had been a huge mistake. How could I go back to school after that?

After washing my face, I stared in the mirror not even recognizing myself. I stepped out of the bathroom pissed the fuck off. Mad at myself for letting Tate play me. Mad that I gave him something so sacred as my virginity and he still shitted on me. I went back to my room grabbed my keys and my coat.

When I got to the stairs, my mom came out of her room. "Where you going?"

"Out." I kept my back to her. My face was swollen from crying. It didn't help that I still had marks from when those bitches jumped me.

"You know you should be grounded, right? Just because you're eighteen and you live with Erin, doesn't mean you can run around here like you ain't got no sense."

I sighed and faced her.

She tied her house coat. "What's wrong with you?" My mama crossed her arms and glowered at me.

"I don't feel good."

"You've been crying." She approached me slowly. "What happened?"

"Tate." I slipped my coat on.

My mama rolled her eyes. "You gon' get enough of chasing that little raggedy ass boy." She shook her head.

"Do you want anything while I'm out?" I started down the stairs.

"Yeah, get me a Dr. Pepper."

I nodded.

"And Erica."

I stopped but didn't turn around.

"Don't let no man break you down." I listened to her footsteps as she walked back to her room.

∼

I PULLED up to Tate's apartment and cut my car off. I stared at his jeep. I then grabbed both new bottles of brake fluid I got at BP gas station. I got out of the car and went to my trunk. Grabbing the Windex, I opened it and emptied the container.

I then refilled it with one bottle of brake fluid. I grabbed the second one and closed the trunk with both bottles in my hands. Once I got to his Jeep, I opened the second bottle and poured it all over the hood. I then sprayed the rest of the car down with the brake fluid in the Windex bottle. After the bottle was done, I went back to my trunk and tossed both bottles in.

I then made my way up to Tate's apartment. I banged on the door until the locks clicked. The door opened, and I came face to face with his sister, Tatem.

"Erica why are you banging on my door like that?" She yawned.

"Where is Tate?" I tried looking past her.

Tatem looked over her shoulder. "He's in his room sleep. He got jumped."

Jumped?

I was taken back by that.

"Some dudes jumped him and robbed him." She stated nonchalantly.

Good

"You wanna come in?"

I walked away from the door and headed back to my car. Once I hopped in and started the ignition, I rested my head against the steering wheel and started crying. As I bawled my eyes out, I wished I'd never met Tate. Our entire relationship had been based on lies. I wasted my time on his immature ass.

After gathering myself, I drove off. Grabbing my phone from the cup holder, I went to my call log. When I got to a stop light, I called Drake and sunk deeper into my seat. I wasn't sure why I needed to talk to him. But I wanted to hear his voice for just a second.

The last thing that should've been on my mind was a male. But Drake was different. He made me feel safe and wanted.

"Wassup, kid?"

"Are you busy?"

"A little. What's good?"

I sniffled. "I just destroyed Tate's paint job."

"Ah, yeah?"

"Yes."

"Where are you now?" He asked me and then told somebody to hold on.

"Driving."

"Where to?"

"I don't know." I didn't want to go back to my Mama's yet, and I wasn't interest in the long drive to the compound.

"Go to the condo and tell Bill I said let you in."

I wiped my face. "Okay."

"Hold on." Drake told me.

I jumped on the highway. I still was in disbelief about the whole Tate situation. I was happy he got his ass beat, but what about the embarrassment I felt? What about my character? He could always repair his car, but he had totaled my reputation.

Drake's end of the phone got loud again. "Erica."

"I'm here."

"Go to the crib. I'll be there later."

"Okay." Tears burned in my eyes. "I'll see you later."

"Aye, Erica..." He sighed. "Stop crying, a'ight? That lil' nigga ain't even worth it, kid."

Warm tears slid down my cheeks.

"Fuck him, a'ight?"

I took deep breath and exhaled slowly to calm myself down.

"You hear me?" He pressed.

"Yeah."

"See you in a minute."

ROME

With my ear plugs in, I wrote in my new journal. I sat comfortably in the corner of the couch. Royal was sitting at the dining room table, cleaning his guns, smoking a blunt. 'The Wood' was playing on the TV even though neither of us were watching it. My eyes bounced to Royal when he stood up.

With his phone to his ear, he went in the kitchen. Since he had an open floor plan, I was able to see him from where I sat. He went in the refrigerator for a quick second and then closed the door. Still on the phone, he walked toward me, holding two bottles of water. I removed my earbuds.

"Nah, I'ma take care of it." Royal told his caller. "You want a water?" He asked me, already extending his hand.

I smiled taking it from him. "Thank you."

I learned quickly that everything Royal did for him, he did for me. Whenever we went somewhere and he had to use the bathroom, he asked me first. He made sure my door was closed before he got in the car. He'd even make me eat if I wasn't hungry. I assumed it was the 'Daddy' in him. For the short amount of time I was around Misa, he had been like that with her too.

He nodded and went back to his seat at the dining room table.

"Shit, I'll probably slide through there in a minute." He paused and then shook his head.

I put my earbuds back in. Royal was always on the go. He rarely ever slept and when he did it wasn't for long. We usually went to sleep together, but if I got up to use the bathroom in the middle of the night, he was gone. It didn't bother me, because every day before I left for work, I got a good dick down.

After taking a well needed sip of water I looked down at the blank page. Since I was a little girl, I always wrote my feelings in a journal. Since I grew up with nobody to confide in, it was the only thing that kept me sane most days. I was writing about my day when a bottle cap dropped down in my lap. Pulling my eyes away from the page, I looked up and over to Royal.

I removed my left earbud. Picking up the bottle cap, I threw it back at him and missed.

He chuckled. "I want some attention." He leaned back in his seat, *still* on the phone.

I laughed. "You're having a whole conversation right now."

Royal shrugged. "I would rather be talking to you."

I smiled. "What do you wanna talk about?"

"Yeah, I just got off the phone with that nigga." He told me to come to him with his index finger.

I closed my journal, tossed it next to me, and got up. When I approached him, Royal pulled me into his lap. He moved my braids out of face and caressed the back of my neck. I closed my eyes.

"You staying the weekend?" He asked me.

You want me to?" Ava didn't have me working. She said if she needed me, we'd meet at her and Twins house.

"Yeah." Royal continued massaging my neck. "I'ma get up wit' you niggas later." He paused. "Yeah, a'ight."

I opened my eyes when I heard his phone land on the table. "You don't get enough sleep."

Royal shrugged. "I don't be tired."

I didn't believe that. "I went through a period where I slept every two days." I admitted. "I had so much on my mental. No matter how much I wrote in my journal to relieve some of the stress, it didn't work."

When I ran my thumb slowly across his furrowed eyebrow, the small wrinkle on his forehead vanished.

"I needed someone to vent to." I switched to his other eyebrow. "Being able to bare your soul to someone every once in a while, is essential."

Royal's hand slid up and down my back. "So, who did you talk to you?"

"God." I stared at him. "I don't go to church every Sunday or read the daily word. But I know he heard me, still does." I massaged the bridge of his nose.

Royal nodded. "I feel you. But I ain't into talking to thin air, Romie Rome." He chuckled. "God been watching me my whole life. He done seen what I been through. I don't need to tell Him some shit He already knows."

"Then tell me." I stared into his dark eyes.

Royal kissed my lips. "I can trust you with my secrets?"

I nodded, gazing into his eyes. "With every last one."

DRAKE

When I stepped inside the crib, it was pitch black. I walked through the darkness and flipped the light switch on. Erica was laid across my black, leather sectional asleep. I walked over, sat down, and placed the jewelry box next to her head.

"Erica." I shook her a little.

She didn't move.

I ran my hand across her head. "Aye..."

Erica opened her puffy eyes slowly and stared up at me. Her glossy eyes danced around me before she sat up all the way and hugged me. Her grip tightened as she cried. Sighing, I hugged her back, patting her back awkwardly. I wasn't into all this emotional shit.

"Stop crying, Erica."

"Why would he do that? Now everybody is talking shit about me."

"So." Erica wasn't the first chick to ever suck a dick. I didn't understand why it was a big deal. In my opinion Tate was in the wrong. What type of bitch ass nigga exposed a chick 'cause she stopped fuckin' with him? These new niggas were weird as fuck.

"People know what I look like naked." She sniffled, getting snot and tears all on my hoodie.

"So..." I shook my head. Erica had ass and titties. Why was that a conversation piece? If a ratchet ass, stripper bitch like Cardi B could get away with it, what was the big fuckin' deal?"

"*Drake*." she pulled away from me whining. "Stop acting like it's not a big deal." Erica wiped her cheeks.

"It's not. You making it one." I shrugged. "Go wash your face." Standing up, I pulled my hoodie over my head.

Erica smacked her lips but headed toward the back. She was stressing over stupid shit. Wasn't no point in crying over something you couldn't change. I trekked to the kitchen and grabbed a can of Pringle's out of the cabinet. A nigga hadn't ate all day, but it didn't hit me 'til just now. I was leaning against the counter eating when Erica rounded the corner.

"I look a hot ass mess." She pressed her face into a towel. "I'm so happy it's Friday." She sighed.

"We burning that towel when you done."

Erica snickered with her face still in the towel.

"My hoodie too. You got booger's all over it."

She laughed. "Leave me alone. I'm sad."

"I don't know what for." I grabbed a Sprite out of the fridge.

Erica hopped onto the counter. "Uh, let's see." She frowned. "Every boy in school knows what I look like sucking dick."

I shrugged. "You ain't the only muthafucka in that school who suck dick."

"But I'm the only one that's currently being exposed and is trending right now." She shot back.

"That's your fault."

Her mug deepened. "How?"

"You chose to fuck with that lame. Now look." I grabbed a few more Pringle's.

"I thought Tate cared about me." She said defensively. "He led me on."

"You let him." I went in my pocket for my ringing phone. "Wassup?" I answered for Tone.

"I just touched down. Meet me at the house."

"A'ight." Ending the call, my gaze landed back on Erica.

"I didn't let him." Erica jumped off the counter as I washed my hands. "Tate told me he loved me."

"And what did he do to show you?" I cut the water off and snatched a paper towel from the holder.

"What?"

I threw the napkin away and walked out of the kitchen with Erica following me closely. *"What did he do to show you he loved you?"* I asked slowly this time. "You keep crying about what he was tellin' you, what about his actions?" We entered my room. "What was he showing you?"

Erica sat quietly on my bed as I searched through my closet for another hoody. I wasn't trying to hurt lil' baby's feelings, but her ass needed a reality check. After deciding on a red and black Gucci hoody, I put it on. When I exited the closet, Erica was still sitting, but I hadn't got an answer yet.

"What you poutin' for now?" Grabbing my phone again, I saw it was Brela, and pressed ignore.

"'Cause you're rude." She got up and threw the washcloth in my dirty clothes hamper.

We left the room with Erica on my heels.

"Every relationship seems perfect when you first start." She said with an attitude.

I made sure I had my keys.

"Tate didn't always act like this."

"Put your shoes on." I told her, ignoring a call from this lil' bitch named Haley. "I won't be here tonight, and I don't want you here by yourself."

Erica stomped to the couch and dropped down. She hopped back up in surprise when she sat on the jewelry box.

"What's this?" She opened it leisurely. A wide smile spread across her face as he eyes danced around what was inside the box. "These are pretty." She stared at the earrings, still grinning. "Thank you, Drake."

I nodded, and she jumped off the couch. Erica wrapped her arms around me, and gazed into my eyes, thanking me once more. Kissing her lips, I squeezed both of her ass cheeks, and pulled her closer to me. I sucked down on her bottom lip and then smacked her ass hard.

"Go put your shoes on."

ROYAL

"Daddy, my mama said I can't spend the night at nobody house." Misa bounced next me. "Why?"

"'Cause it ain't good for you to sleepover other people house."

"Why?"

"'Cause you could get sick."

She skipped up the steps and to the front door. "How?"

"Germs." I unlocked the door and pushed it open.

"Oh." She nodded as I closed the door and sat her overnight bag down. "So, why can I stay here?"

Frowning, I led the way through the townhouse. "You live here, Misa."

"I thought I lived with my mama."

"You live with both of us."

"But I sleep in the bed at my mama's house. I only sleep in the bed at your house sometimes."

I stopped walking and looked down at her. "Just because you only here sometimes don't mean this ain't yo house."

She looked up at me.

"Everything in here is yours." I rubbed the top of her head.

"Ok." Misa said innocently.

I never wanted my seed to feel like my home wasn't hers. I didn't get to see Misa as much as her mama did, but I loved her just as much. From the outside looking in, I'm sure most thought I was a 'part-time' father. I couldn't just sit around house, though. My family had to eat.

"Erica, I just gave you my password to Instagram and Facebook. Why do you need my Snapchat, too." Rome's voice sounded off from downstairs in the second living room area.

Misa stopped walking. "Daddy, somebody is in your house."

"I know." I heard a dog bark. Rome brought Grizzy B even though I told her not.

"And a dog!" Misa ran down the steps and I followed slowly. "*Awwwww.*" Misa cooed. "Look at the little puppy."

I chuckled at her.

Grizzy B barked.

"Erica let me call you right back." Rome stood up. "No, Erica." She laughed. "Later."

"Hi, Rome." Misa waved.

Rome smiled. "Hi, Misa."

"Is this your dog?"

"Yep. That's Grizzy B."

Shaking my head, I took a seat on the couch. "What I tell you about that mutt?"

Rome snickered before scooping Grizzy B up. "Griselda. You hear him talking about you?"

"I thought his name was Grizzy B." Misa held her arms out for the dog.

"That's her nickname. Her real name is Griselda Blanco."

Rome's ass had to be high when she named the dog that. Grizzy B looked like a walking white puff ball. She was always barking and running around.

"It's a 'her'?" Misa rubbed Grizzy's head.

"Mmhm..."

"Can I take her outside?"

"Misa I thought you was hanging with Daddy?" Laying my head back against the sofa, I closed my eyes.

"I can later. I wanna go now before Grizzy B and Rome go home." Misa sat the dog down and she took off.

"Rome and Grizzy are spending the night." The room got quiet as fuck. I had to open my eyes to make sure I wasn't alone. My gaze landed on Misa and she was frowning.

"Wassup, Mini me?"

"Rome ain't gon' get sick?" Misa looked Rome up and down, and then back to me. I had to stifle a smile, 'cause she reminded me of her mama when she did that.

"Nah."

"I thought it wasn't good to sleep over other people house. Rome don't live here." In a matter of seconds Misa went from liking Rome, to not feeling her presence; it was written all over her face.

"Rome lives here sometimes."

Misa mugged me. "More than me?"

My kid was fonkin'. "No Mini me, nobody lives here more than you." Leaning forward on my elbows, I motioned for her to come to me.

She stomped the entire way.

"Misa this is your house. Daddy promises to do better so you can come live here more." Misa was the most important person in my life. Her feeling like this let me know I was slacking as a father. I couldn't have my Mini me out here feeling second to my lifestyle.

Misa looked up at Rome. "Okay." She sighed.

I stretched my arms out for a hung and she fell into my chest.

"Rome can I take Grizzy B outside?" Misa pushed off me.

"If it's okay with your dad." Rome answered and then looked down at me.

"You can go in the backyard." Since it was fenced in I knew her and Grizzy B couldn't run off.

Misa picked up a little windbreaker jacket. "Rome can we put this on her?"

"Yep. She's going to need it." They walked back upstairs with Misa asking if she could dress Gizzy B up and take pictures.

Resting back into the couch, I closed my eyes. I planned on dropping Misa's bag off and taking them to get food, but if they weren't hungry right now, I was gon' give them time and space to bond.

11

THE END OF SOMETHING GOOD?

ERICA

Social media is the devil. I had to log out of my accounts and log into Rome's because of all the tags I was getting. People I didn't even know where judging me and calling me everything but a child of God. I wanted to surf the internet without all the drama, and Rome's page was perfect for that. She had a bunch of friends and followers but never posted anything.

I scrolled down her timeline lying across Erin's bed. She wasn't feeling too good, and kept complaining about feeling nauseous She'd been lying in bed all day falling asleep off and on. Toni and Sanaa were with Sadee since it was the weekend and she wanted all the kids. Tone as always, was gone, and Rome was with Royal.

I was shocked Tate hadn't called me to cuss me out about his car. If I would've had something hard enough, he wouldn't have had windows in that bitch either. I told Erin all about everything that happened, including the shit at the restaurant. She told me if I took him back we were going to square up. Her crazy ass was dead serious because she didn't crack a smile when she said it.

"Every time I see you, you got on new jewelry." Erin yawned.

I smiled, still being nosey on Instagram.

"Drake got you blushing like that?"

Shrugging, I turned on my side. "He's cool, it ain't nothing like that." In all honesty, I didn't know what the hell was going on between me and Drake.

Erin smacked her lips. "Girl, please. It's something. You sitting here chillin in a bust-down Rollie, tennis bracelet and necklace, and new earrings. She chuckled. "I already see where this is going."

I won't lie and say I didn't like the jewelry. I could see why Drake wore so much of it. I looked fly as fuck and I felt like a boss. My makeup was beat, and since I let my hair air dry, I pulled it up into a crinkly bun. I looked too cute to be sitting in the house with Erin's pregnant ass. But I loved my sissy so she had company…for now.

She thought nobody knew, but I did. She was sleeping all the time, cranky, and constantly snacking. I hoped this time she got a boy.

"And where is it going, Erin Morris?" I still couldn't believe she was married to Tone. The phat ass rock on her finger probably cost more than everything I had on.

Erin adjusted her pillow. "You're going to end up falling in love."

"I'm done with love." I looked back down at my phone. "Fuck these niggas, sis."

She laughed. "Okay, *sis*. Give it time. At the rate y'all going it'll happen one day."

"One day…maybe."

Drake was fresh out of prison. He wasn't thinking about me. That nigga was probably fucking everything with a pussy. He could go hours without talking to me. Even when I texted him he took forever to get back to me.

"Erica just be careful, okay. Dudes like Drake come with a lot of baggage." She warned.

Baggage? Didn't we all come with some type of problems? "Erin, I'm a big girl. I'm freshly out of a relationship. The last thing on my mind is trying to please another man." I would consider the shit I was going through with Tate a traumatic experience.

Erin stared at me like she didn't believe me. And if I was being completely honest, I didn't know who I was trying to convince...me or her.

"Don't look at me like that." I looked back down at my phone.

"Just be careful."

"Mmm hmm..." I was about to log out of Rome's Instagram, when she got an inbox. Seeing it was a video message from some chick, I pressed play.

The video started, and it wasn't nothing but somebody recording their burger and then the camera shifted to Royal. They looked like they were at 'Freddy's'. Royal didn't even know he was being recorded. When Myka's face appeared on the screen, my heart dropped. Since the video was from Snapchat the caption read "Eating for two again".

Immediately, I exited out of the app. I jumped up from Erin's bed and started out of her room, dialing Rome.

"Well, bye to you too!" Erin called out.

I chucked the deuces up just as Rome answered the phone.

"Erica..." she laughed. "Hold on. Move Royal. I'm serious." She cracked up. "Stop. Erica, what's up?"

"Rome...Myka is pregnant."

ROME

The smile I'd once been sporting left my face as my glare burned a whole through the back of Royal's head.

"Rome, did you hear me?"

I didn't even hang up the phone before I threw it at Royal. It smacked him hard causing his hand to fly to his head. He spun around and faced me with a mean mug. "The fuck is wrong wit' you?"

"Is Myka pregnant?"

Royal tossed the PS4 controller next to him. "Rome."

"Don't *Rome* me." Crossing my arms against my chest, I inched toward him at a snail's pace. I knew that if I moved too fast there was a likely chance I'd steal on his ass. I wasn't into that domestic violence shit. "*Is...Myka...Pregnant?*"

He stood up. "Yeah."

Closing my eyes, I took a deep breath. As I exhaled, I thought about all the shit I'd been through that was much worse than this. It was a technique I used to calm myself down. My life had been full of uphill battles and brutal punishments. I had to remind myself this was simply a slap on the wrist.

When I opened my eyes, I spun around and left the room. "Fuck you, Royal."

"Rome." He followed after me. "Don't you wanna hear a nigga out."

That was really code for 'let me tell you this lie to make you feel better'. "Nope." Shrugging, I climbed the stairs. "I need to get my things out of your room."

Royal trekked behind me in silence. We walked past Misa's room and she was still dressing Grizzy B up.

"Rome, look." She jumped up with Grizzy B in her arms. She was dressed in a pink rain coat, with matching booties. Misa cheesed as Grizzy struggled to jump out of her arms.

I stopped walking and laughed. "Awww Griselda, you look cute." Despite me not feeling her daddy right now, Misa hadn't done anything to me. There was no way I was going to take my anger out on her or Grizzy B.

Misa smiled harder. "Ain't she pretty? Can I send a picture to my mama?"

I looked over and up at Royal. His expression was unreadable, but he nodded, passing Misa his phone. Once she ran back off into her room, I started for Royal's again.

"You ain't tryna hear shit I gotta say." He had the nerve to sound mad.

"Because you're going to lie." The first thing I grabbed was my journal off the dresser. "Plus, you have a whole family, Royal."

"I got two kids."

"Congratulations."

Royal grabbed my arm and made me face him. "Myka is three months pregnant Rome. It was before us."

"So, I'm supposed to just sit back and watch you play house with her?" I didn't want to cry, but my feelings were crushed; I really liked Royal.

He rubbed the back of his neck. "I'm not playing house with Myka. She knows what it is." Royal looked just as defeated as I felt.

"And what is it?"

"Something that shouldn't have happened."

"That you can't take back..." I went back to gathering my things.

"I don't want Myka."

"And I don't want you." I shot back out of anger.

"What do you want me to do, Rome?"

"Leave me alone, please."

"Nah." He came up behind me and wrapped his arms around me. "I don't want Myka." He repeated. "And she knows that."

I smacked my lips.

"The shit happened before we met. I ain't been fucking her."

He's lying.

I tried to pull away from him.

"I told her to get an abortion. When you asked me about it, I really thought she handled it." I had never heard Royal's voice sound so soft and desperate. "She lied."

"So why didn't you tell me?"

"I didn't know how to."

I attempted to pull away again.

"I should've told you. It was wrong to keep it a secret from you, but in my defense, she just told me this week, shorty."

"This won't work, Royal."

"Why? Cause you don't want it to?"

Can you believe the nerve of this nigga? He had the baby on the way, not me. "You're about to have a baby with someone who is still in love with you." I didn't need that drama in my life. Call me selfish, but I was still trying to figure out *Rome*. I was going through a lost identity phase. Half the time I didn't know if I was coming or going.

"I'm not in love with Myka."

Were all men stupid? "Royal let me go."

"Tell me we can work it out and I will."

I couldn't believe this fool was giving *me* an ultimatum, when *he* was having the kid.

"I wanna be wit' you, Romie Rome."

Rolling my eyes, I sighed deeply.

"I know you wanna be wit' a nigga too."

Cocky ass.

"Look..." Royal turned me around. "I'll let you go to put some space between us for a few days."

I looked up at him like he was basket case. That had to be the only reason he wasn't understanding the words that were coming out of my mouth.

"Leave you and Grizzy B shit here, and when you come back home, we can talk about it."

"Ho—" I pierced my lips. Royal refused to comprehend what I was telling him. "You know what..." With my journal still in hand, I stormed out of his room to get Griselda so we could leave.

DRAKE

♫ *"Says Chanel on her purse, she ain't playing with these hoes*
I need head, lick my blunt, she keep playing on the pole
What you knew? what you know? Girl, you got a body
Private show, she gon show after 9-5
I just wanna lay you up, I just wanna lay some pipe" ♫

Half-naked bitches were sliding up and down poles, walking around ass naked begging for lap dances, and some were even fuckin' each other. I held a bottle of D'usse in my right hand and I blunt in my left. A couple stacks of cash sat in my lap as my eyes swept the room. Tone had a bitch all in his face begging to go home with him. Shorty was barking up the wrong tree, that nigga had been on some weird faithful shit.

When we first got to the strip club an hour ago, he said he was leaving before us. E wasn't feeling good and even though she told him it was cool if hung he with the boys, he wanted to go be up under her. Shit, I wasn't hating. If I was gon' keep it completely one hundred, I had been texting Erica. The only problem was her ass not hitting me back.

Her little ass had me checking my phone every few minutes. Tone stood up dapped me and a couple of the homies up and then bounced. True was still going hard, talking shit to a bitch who made herself way too comfy in our section. Everybody was laughing at her dumb ass, and I'm guessing since she knew True's pockets were long, the hoe laughed right along with us.

I passed the blunt off to Lucus, grabbed the cash in my lap, and stood up to leave.

"You out too?" True threw two bills at ole girl. "Bye, shorty." He dismissed her.

Nodding, I walked out of the section, through the joint and outside. I removed my phone from my coat pocket. Taking another hit out of the bottle, I approached my car and sat it down on the ground. I pulled up Erica's name, called and leaned against my whip. When she answered the phone she was telling Rome to stop mugging her because she didn't do nothing to her.

I chuckled.

"Hello."

"What you doin', kid?"

She smacked her lips. "My name is not 'kid' Drake. I keep telling you to stop calling me that." Erica felt like I was taking a jab at her age when I called her that. And I was. She was eight years younger than me. I wasn't bothered by the gap, though.

"What you' doin'?"

"Talking to Rome about you niggas."

Shaking my head, I hopped into my car. "Why you keep groupin' me wit' them niggas?" Erica sounded like one of them man bashing, bitter bitches.

"'Cause y'all are irritating."

"You bouta get you a girlfriend?" I peeled out of the parking lot.

Erica laughed. "No, fool. I'm taking a break from y'all, though."

"Me too?"

"What makes you so special?" She scoffed. "'Cause you bought me jewelry?"

"That shit was light work, kid."

"Mmhm."

The line went quiet for a minute and then...

"Drake are you married?"

I chuckled. "Nah."

"Got a girlfriend?"

"Nope."

"A baby on the way?"

"Not that I know of." I shrugged.

"I'm serious."

"No Erica, I ain't got no wife, bitch, or no shorties." I clarified.

She told Rome I was probably lying, and she got a genuine laugh out of me. Erica was naïve as fuck, but she was outspoken. She was shallow sometimes, but she was grounded in all the right places.

"Why you callin' me a liar? Where you at?" I hopped on the highway towards my condo.

"Home."

"You should lay up wit' me." Running a red light, I raced down the highway.

"Lay up?"

"Yeah. I wanna fuck you wit' all that ice I know you got on."

She laughed, and she must've had me on speaker because it sounded like Rome joined in. "I'm not having sex with you again, Drake." Erica stated in a tone I wasn't feeling.

"Why not?"

"Because if I give you some and I don't hear from you for a couple days, I'ma come to your apartment and break everything in there."

I laughed 'cause I believed her little rowdy ass. "So that's how you do me? You gon' leave me hanging?"

"Yep." She popped the 'p'. "So, call one of them thotties in your phone. Or better yet." She chuckled condescendingly. "Call that chick who showed up with that Chinese food."

Touché...

"You ain't my man Drake. We kicked it on Valentine's Day, but don't make it seem more than that. Because I know it's not." She said flatly. "When I want some dick, I'll call you." She hung up in my face.

Did this bitch just Jodi me...

"Lil' savage ass."

ROYAL

I pulled up to my parent's house with Misa rambling about how cute Grizzy B looked in her clothes still. After Rome left last night, I sat around the crib. I wanted to be with her but if my seed was gone be a problem, then maybe we didn't need to be together. Rome being mad at me didn't bother me because I expected that. I just didn't have time for her to be treating my shorty some type of way because she didn't fuck with Myka.

"Daddy, Grandma said we baking a cake today." Misa said as I helped her out of my whip. "Are you gon' eat some cake?"

Nodding, I shut her door and she took off running. My mother, Gia, was standing in the doorway. A big smiled graced her face as she waited on Misa to get to her. My mother was the prettiest I'd ever seen. And I wasn't just saying that cause she birthed me. She had a smooth, dark chocolate complex, big, bright eyes, little button nose, and perfect, white teeth.

My mother was in her early sixties, but she looked like she was more in her late forties. Since she didn't work, she stayed active other ways. She gardened, worked out twice a week, volunteered at her church, and occasionally couponed with her old ass friends if they weren't at bingo. I couldn't remember the last time Gia Henshaw held down a job. She never went without, though. And I would never let her.

"Misa!" She squealed. "Hi, baby. You look so pretty."

Misa wrapped her arms around my mother's waist. "Hi Grandma." They shared a tight embrace before Misa took off into the house.

My mother crossed her arms and looked me up and down as I climbed the stairs. "Well, well, well. Look who finally decided to come see their mother. I'm glad to see you're still alive." She side eyed me.

I pulled her into a hug and she smacked her lips. "Wassup, Ma."

"Royal, I'm serious." She patted my back with both of her hands and then gave me a firm squeeze. "I've been worried about you. Luna said she told you I was looking for you." She pulled away from me. "I hate when you stay away like that."

"I know." I looked down at my favorite lady.

My mama stared at me intently. The intensity in her gaze reminded me of when I was kid. "Your father has been asking about you too."

I nodded.

"Come on." She went in the house and stepped to the side to let me in. "You hungry? Has Misa ate?"

"Yeah, we just left 'Go Chicken Go'."

My mama shut the door and I followed her to the family room. My moms and pops still lived on the block I was raised on. That was part of the reason it was so hard to leave the streets alone. Even though I offered to uproot them, they wouldn't. Well, Willard Henshaw wouldn't. My father worked for the city and drove a garbage truck. He had been working there my whole life.

I was probably his least favorite child, and I didn't give a fuck. Which was why I always stayed away. He couldn't accept I was a street nigga, so he treated me differently. Shit, what did he expect? It wasn't like I was raised in the best conditions.

"Willard, look who came to see us." My mama smiled, patting my back gently.

He looked up from the book he was reading.

"Wassup, Pop." I tilted my head.

"Son." He looked back down at his book. "How are you?"

"I'm straight." I sat down on the couch.

"You thirsty?" My mama asked.

"Nah."

"You sure, Royal?" She pressed. When I nodded, she sighed. "What about you honey?"

"I'm fine."

Shaking her head, she started out of the living room. "Let me go see what Misa is doing."

"Ma." I leaned back and laid my arms out across the top of the sofa. "Can you watch Misa until the morning? I got some shit I gotta take care of."

"Su—"

"Is that why you came here? To ask you mama to take care of your responsibility?"

I looked up at the ceiling.

"Willard don't—"

"Gia go find my granddaughter." He snapped, cutting her off. "Let me talk to Royal."

Opening my eyes, I leaned forward placing my elbows on my knees. I clasped my hands and hung my head.

"Royal, your mother is not a daycare provider. You can't even check in with her from time to time, but you want her to do you favors."

"All I did was ask a question." I lifted my head to stare at him. "She ain't gotta watch Misa if she don't want to."

"But you know she will." He frowned. "And if she doesn't, my granddaughter will end up with Luna or Myka's father, while you're out running the streets." His voice rose.

"Running the streets to take care of her."

"You can provide for Misa without being a street thug, Royal. When I named you that, I wanted you to live up to your name." His pointed finger rose up and down as he glared at me. "You weren't raised to be...this."

"Paid?"

"Son, you've sold your soul to the devil. And for what? Money, cars, and clothes? What about principle, what about morals, and values?" Pops dropped his book in his lap. "When I look at you, it's like I don't even know who you are anymore."

"Cause you ain't lookin at me..." I frowned. "You judging me."

"Where did I go wrong, Royal?" He said, disappointed. "I worked, your mother was always here." His eyes roamed me. "Why are you like this? You curse in front of your mother and daughter, you're constantly getting shot up."

Ah, so that's what this conversation was about. They heard about me getting hit up.

"You sell drugs, and I noticed the gun on your hip the minute you waltzed in here."

"I wasn't trying to hide it." I shrugged.

"See?" He jumped up from his seat. "Do you hear yourself?"

I stood up too. "I'm out. Ma! You got Misa?"

"I wasn't done talking to you Royal." Pop spoke, but I was already making my way towards the exit.

My mama and Mini me came rushing to the front of the house. "You leaving already, Royal?"

"Bye, daddy!"

"I'll be back tomorrow." I hugged my mama. "Mini me, I'ma pick you up in the morning for breakfast." Picking her up, I kissed the top of her head, gave her a tight squeeze, and then put her down on her feet.

"He's running again, Gia." My pops called from the living room.

I quickly kissed the top of Ma Duke's forehead and left.

12

LISTEN TO YOUR HEART

ERICA

I left out of my job interview at Applebee's, and even though the meeting lasted all of fifteen minutes, I got it. The manager said he liked my smile and then handed me the uniform. His name was Nash, and he told me to be back the next day to fill out paperwork. I was doing this because I promised E I would, but I couldn't guarantee employment over one week.

Once I was secure in my seatbelt, I started my car. The night before, Drake called me and even though I wanted to see him, I refused to be left looking stupid. So, why was I thinking about going to his house? And after that, why did I head there? I didn't even bother calling.

When I got there, the doorman let me up. I was just about to knock on Drake's door when it opened. Chinese chick stepped out and jumped in surprise at the sight of me. She grabbed her imaginary pearls and stared me up and down. Drake appeared next, with a smirk that was about to make me drop kick his ass.

"Hey." She smiled and had the nerve to hold her hand out.

I stared at Drake. "I need to talk to you."

"Brela, I'ma get wit' you later."

Oh, yeah?

I chuckled.

"Okay, see ya." She walked past me and then scurried down the hall.

Drake stared down at me. He didn't have on a shirt, so his tattoos were jumping out at me like pop art. As usual, he had all his jewelry on, and gray sweats that had his dick print looking like a photoshopped picture. His mannish ass grabbed his crouch, ran his tongue across his bottom grill, and then licked his lips. Drake tilted his head to the side and smiled.

"Wassup, kid."

Pushing past him, I let myself in. "You're a whore." His condo was spotless.

"What you want?" He wrapped his arms around me and then kissed the side of my face.

I tried to elbow him, but he jumped back. "Don't put your lips on me." Spinning around, I eyed him up and down. "I don't know where your mouth has been."

"On this sandwich." He walked past me and to the dining room. Drake sat down at the table in front of a plate containing a large burger and fries.

Squinting my eyes at him, I placed my Chanel bag down on the table. "After you called me, you called her?" I watched him take his grill out and sit it down on a napkin.

What is wrong with this nigga?

Why would he think that's okay? I knew what I said on the phone but come on! I thought maybe he went home and fell asleep or ran the streets all night. But nope. This fool invited a chick over and fucked her.

I looked around the room for something to break.

"Nah, she came over to check on me." He nonchalantly ate his burger.

"What?"

"She saw me come in sick this morning. Since I helped her with her car, she helped me. She's a doctor." He chewed, unbothered as he stared down at his phone.

"A doctor? You expect me to believe that?"

Drake shrugged. "What you do today?"

I stared at him real hard. A few seconds passed and when I realized he wasn't going to look up at me, I crossed my arms.

"Went to a job interview." I took a seat at the table, still staring at him.

Drake looked up at me with those funny colored eyes. "You get it?"

"Yep. I'm a little nervous, though. I've never had to take my clothes off in a room full of people."

"What?" He stopped eating.

"I'm stripping now. I'm supposed to be there at midnight."

Drake's face dropped, and his eyes went black. Even though he looked scary as shit, I laughed.

"I'm just playing. It's a waitress position at Applebee's."

"That shit ain't funny."

"Awww, you were in your feelings." I smiled. "You like me a little."

"I like you a lot." He finished off the rest of his food.

"I know you had sex with her." His ass wasn't getting off that easily.

Drake leaned back in his chair. "I know I didn't." He smiled. "I like yo hair and makeup like that."

I tried not to smile, I swear I did, but the corners of my mouth lifted slowly. "Thank you."

"No problem." He winked at me quickly.

We stared at each other quietly. Our eyes would occasionally roam over one another, but then they'd lock again. I'm not sure how long we did that, but when his phone sounded off, it ended. Drake answered his phone and sighed.

"Wassup?"

I got up from my seat. "I'm gone." He didn't even bother getting up when I grabbed my purse.

"I'ma get wit' you later, kid. A'ight?"

Ignoring him, I let myself out. When I shut the door, Chinese chick was walking past me in blue scrubs. She waved to me with her phone to her ear before stopping at the elevator.

"Yeah girl. I'm running late to the hospital, I overslept."

ROME

Twin agreed to take my car to get new tires, so after we ate lunch with Ava, we headed to Tonio's body shop. I was excited because never in my life did I think I'd be spending ten thousand dollars on tires. Tires. But here we were chilling in Tonio's office. He was at home with Erin but gave me and Twin the key to his space.

I sat behind his desk, taking it all in. My brothers were some fuckin' bosses. Everybody that was surrounded by them was paid. Nobody acted snaky or seemed fake either. Their whole camp was a buncha criminals or killers, though.

"How long have you and Ava been together?" I broke the silence.

Twin, who was rolling up a blunt, shrugged. "A minute."

"She's cool." My first week with Ava had been successful. She was bossy, and talked more shit than a little, but every day was an adventure. I liked Ava, and she was a good look for my brother.

"Her ass is crazy." He took a seat in a free chair in front of the desk. "But that's my love."

I smiled. It was crazy how a couple months I didn't even know I had brothers. Now here they were, spoiling me and giving me opportunities to advance in life. Me and Twin had the same mom and dad, so our looks were a little more identical. The only difference was our skin tones.

Macie, our mother was a dead beat. She didn't even raise Twin; Sadee, Tonio's mother did. I'd seen her one time since I'd been here. She showed up crying and being dramatic, trying to get me to talk to her. I planned on sitting down with her and having an open conversation, I just didn't know when.

"Have you talked to Macie lately?" I asked curiously.

Twin blew smoke from his nostrils. "Like two days ago."

I nodded. "Are y'all close?"

He frowned. "Nah."

"Do you wanna be close with her?" We both grew up without both parents. The only difference was he was raised by Macie's family. I was the outcast, the black sheep.

Twin passed me the weed. "Not for real. I tolerate her ass out of respect for Auntie."

I laughed. Sadee was everybody's fairy Godmother. Even I had taken to her. She texted me every morning and she told me loved me every night. I'm sure if I'd grown up with her in my life, I'd be much more different.

"You wanna sit down wit' her or somethin'?"

I shook my head no. "Not really." At least not right now. I needed to get my own shit together before I endured Macie's.

Twin stared at me. "I know how you feel."

"Do you?" My head shifted slightly. "You know how it feels to grow up lonely?" My face hardened. "You know how it feels to have nobody you can trust? No friends, family...nothing?"

I wasn't trying to take my hurt out on Roman, but our parents were the cause of all my pain. They got rid of me. Left me with strangers. Made me feign for myself, leaving me broken. I believed in forgiveness because everyone made mistakes, but I wasn't mature enough to have a conversation with Macie just yet.

"Nah, but I know how it feels to not have a moms and pops." He shrugged taking the blunt from me.

"Did you cry a lot?" I pulled my legs into the chair and crossed them.

Twin stared at me for a few seconds. "I cried every day until I was seven." He licked his lips before taking a long pull. When he exhaled, he cleared his throat. "You gotta let that hurt go, though."

I frowned.

"That shit ain't doing nothin' but holding you back." Twin shrugged again. "You bright as fuck, Rome. Don't let Macie or no nigga dim you down, shorty."

I smiled. "Thanks, Twin."

He nodded. "You gon' be a'ight. You here now and we got you."

Hearing that settled my nerves. Regardless of what me and Royal was going through, my brothers were in my corner. They were the only people I could see myself ever truly trusting. Tonio and Twin were the only men I'd ever met who looked out for me and didn't expect anything in return. They went out of their way to show me they loved me. I felt secure around them.

Relaxing into my seat, I let what he said register. God had definitely blessed me. Me and Twin chilled in Tonio's office after that learning each other's likes and dislikes. He was more lax then Tonio, and he smiled way more too. Twin made me swear to have lunch with him every Monday no matter what.

Once my car was ready, we went our separate ways. Royal ran across my mind and I quickly put him to the back of it. Me and Grizzy B still had clothes at his house. I knew that if I went to get them, he'd try to talk me into hearing his bullshit ass excuses. Deciding against it, I headed back to Ava's shop to see if she needed me.

DRAKE

"Oh my God!" Erica crossed her arms to cover her titties. "What are you doing?"

"What you covering up for?" I smirked before taking a bite out of a green apple.

"What is wrong with you?" She continued rinsing soap off her body.

Too bad we were at Tone and Erin's cause I wanted to jump in the shower and beat the pussy up. Watching the suds wash down her curves and into the crack of her ass made me grab my dick. The tattoo on her back was of different phases of the moon going down her spine. When she reached to cut the water off, I slapped her ass making it jiggle.

"Is there a reason you're in here?" She wrapped her towel around her body and stepped out. "Shouldn't you be at home eating dinner with your doctor?"

After throwing the rest of my apple in the trash can, I followed her out of her En-suite bathroom. "I came to chill for a minute."

"I don't have a minute, Drake."

"Why not, *Erica*?" Sitting down on her bed I removed my piece from my hip and sat it on the nightstand.

After she dried herself off, she dropped her towel. "Because I'm tired. I have to be up early for school to tutor and I start my job tomorrow." I watched as she went in her drawer. "I probably won't get back home until after ten."

I nodded, laying onto my back. "A'ight." Erica's bed was soft as fuck.

"Drake?" She flopped down on the bed.

"Wassup."

"What are you doing here?"

Opening my eyes, I looked over at her. "Tone needed me to come through."

Erica rolled her eyes in irritation "No. I mean why are you in my room? I'm not having sex with you in my sister's house."

"I didn't come up here to fuck." I wasn't gon' disrespect my fam like that. Plus, Roman was downstairs waiting on me.

She smacked her lips. "Then why did you bust in on me in the shower?"

"Just cause I ain't gettin' the pussy, don't mean I can't see it."

Erica gave me the side-eye. "That's exactly what that means, fool."

I don't know what kind of voodoo Erica put on me on Valentine's Day. Nigga only got the pussy once and I was hounding the broad. She was the only chick who could get me to text back and forth all day. Yeah sometimes I replied a little late but that's only cause I was always moving around.

"Why you trying to play hard to get?"

Erica stared at me for a second before she burst out laughing. "*Hard to get*. Because I don't wanna have sex with you? Why are you so conceited?"

"I already got the pussy, I don't know what you holding out for." Erica had me buying jewelry, leaving the strip club to call her, and popping up to check in with her on some creep shit. And I let her get snot and tears on one of my favorite hoodies. I knew she was a problem when I let her sit in my crib without me.

"Drake I just got out of a bad relationship. Can I get over that hurt first?"

I frowned. "The fuck you hurt for?" Erica was too good of a chick for a bum like Tate. She wasn't like other young, dumb high school kids. She was high maintenance as fuck, and I respected that because that meant she knew her worth. Shit, to be honest, she was probably too good for a nigga like me.

"Uhh, le'ts see..." she crossed her legs. "My first real boyfriend just exposed me to the entire student body."

"You still trippin' off that?"

"Yes!" She shrieked. "Why wouldn't I be? Drake, he embarrassed me. If I could drop out, I would. Thank God graduation is coming up."

I shook my head.

"I *really* thought he loved me. "

"Why? You didn't even *really* love him."

"Yes, I did."

"Then why did we fuck?"

Erica opened her mouth to speak but nothing came out.

"If you loved that lil nigga you wouldn't have gave the pussy up for revenge."

Her eyes widened at my truth.

"That was puppy love, kid. I'm on some grown man shit."

She gazed at me. "You just had a chick at your condo. Why are trying to game me down." Erica chuckled. "Why can't you just be up front. Just say '*Erica, you got the best pussy I've ever had. Can I have some more, please?*'"

I folded my hands behind my head and closed my eyes. "Shit, if all I had to do was ask nicely..."

She laughed. "No, but for real. Stop lying to me. If you're really interested like you say you are then we should take it slow."

"Which means no sex?" I slid one hand in my Versace briefs.

"Not for awhile."

"Do I get my dick sucked."

Erica hit my arm. "Hell no."

"Can I still eat the pussy?"

"Yep."

I opened my eyes. "What kinda shit is that?"

She cracked up. "Quit fronting like you're really going to go without sex and head."

Raising up, I rotated my shoulders, and popped my neck. "I might."

"Not."

I chuckled, standing up. "You too smart for your own good, kid."

As I tucked my burner back in my jeans, Erica snuggled underneath her cover. "Bye, Drake."

Frowning, I hovered over her, resting my palms on the bed. "I don't get a good night kiss?"

She puckered her lips and I planted a soft kiss on them. Leaving her room, I checked the time on my phone and saw it was almost eleven.

"Sleep tight, kid." I called over my shoulder.

ROYAL

Me: Come outside or I'ma come knock on the door
   Rome: I told you if you didn't have me and GB's clothes I wasn't coming out.
   I turned my car off.
   Me: Ok
   Getting out, I shut the door and flipped my hoodie over my head. As I was climbing the steps the door opened and Drake and Roman came out.
   "What's good, nigga." I slapped fives with Drake.
   "Same ole." We locked B's. "I came to rap wit' Rome." I dapped up Roman.
   He titled his head, frowning. "About what?"
   "No disrespect OG, but that's between me and her."
   Drake smirked before walking around me. "I know that nigga True been waiting on us."
   Roman grilled me.
   "I just came to talk."
   He looked back at the house just as the door opened and Tone stepped out.
   "Wassup." He tossed his chin up.

"What up, OG." We locked B's.

"This nigga here to see Rome."

Tone mugged me. "Rome who?"

"Morris." Drake chuckled from behind me.

"What you need wit' my sister?"

"I need to talk to her."

Roman sucked his teeth. "About what?"

I stared at him. I just told this nigga it was none of his fuckin' business. This was me and Rome's relationship. Not me, Rome, Tone, and Roman. I respected both of them, but this ain't have shit to do with money, so I didn't have to answer to them. So, I wasn't.

The door opened again, and Rome appeared. "Really, Royal."

"You coming home tonight or what?"

"*Home*?" Tone faced her. "The fuck is he talkin' bout, Rome?"

She crossed her arms. "I've been spending the night at Royals."

"Man..." Roman drawled. "Baby sis, come on."

"I'm grown Roman. And I have needs."

"Rome." Tone gave her a hard look. "Don't nobody wanna hear all that, man."

Drake laughed.

"What?" She shrugged.

"You said you been staying with Ma Duke." Tone tugged at his beard. "You a liar now?"

"No. I just didn't know how to tell you I was seeing Royal."

"When you say *see*..." Roman looked back and forth between me and Rome. "You mean see, see? Like..." He frowned and Drake laughed harder.

"Sex?" Rome asked nonchalantly. "Yes."

Roman stepped down the stairs. "I'm out." He shook his head.

"How long this been going on? You been fuckin' in my crib?" Tone stared down at Rome.

She grimaced. "No! And It's none of your business who I'm sleeping with. I'll be twenty in less than two months."

Tone nodded. "We'll talk later." He faced me. "Come holler at me, youngin'." He went back into the house.

Rome gave me a "see what you did" look and followed after him. Once I was inside, she shut the door. "Damn it, Royal. Why are so stubborn?"

"Cause you trippin' wit' me over nothin'."

She scowled. "Royal! You have a baby on the way!"

"What that gotta do with us, Rome? I'm not with Myka. I'm not fuckin' Myka, and once my seed get here that won't change."

She sighed.

"Hey, Royal." Erin approached us with a bag of popcorn.

"Sup, E."

"Y'all good?" She looked at Rome first and they shared a look that was unreadable.

Rome nodded. "Yeah, Tonio wants to talk to Royal."

Erin smiled. "I told him to play nice, so he'll be fine." She headed for the stairs. "He's in his office." Erin called over shoulder before climbing the steps.

Rome smacked her lips. "Come on." She led the way through the mansion quietly. When we got to the double doors of Tone's office, Rome sighed again. "Please just be cool."

I frowned. "Rome, I work with this nigga every day. I'm feeling you shorty, but it ain't that deep." I wasn't dying for no broad.

She snickered and then punched me in my arm. "Asshole."

"You coming home tonight." I knocked twice on the door before stepping in. Tone was sitting behind his desk doing something on his iMac. He motioned for me to come all the way in before drinking from a double Styrofoam cup.

"Sit down, Royal."

I took a seat and leaned back.

"My baby sister been here for what? Two months now? So, I'm just assume y'all been fuckin' for a minute." He stared at me. "She's old enough to make her own choices and since she's decided to fuck wit' you, I'ma just say this. Don't make me kill you, Royal."

I titled my head.

"I trust you with my wife's life almost every day. So, I know Rome is in good hands, but keep my sister away from the hood."

I nodded.

"The first time she comes to me crying, I'ma kill you, Royal." Tone had hazel eyes, but them shits always dimmed to a light brown when he was in murder man mode. He was giving me the same look he gave niggas before he put a bullet in their dome.

Again, I nodded. There was nothing left to be said. Tone wasn't the type of nigga to give second chances. I stood and dapped him up.

"I'ma get wit' you later, youngin'."

"Fa'sho." I left his office. As I was shutting the door, Rome switched toward me. She had her coat on and Grizzy B in her arms.

"Can we stop and get food first?"

13

GIRLS NEED LOVE TOO
ERICA

I got through my first week of work with a breeze. Drake brought me lunch every day and popped up to my job twice. He was getting better at texting too.

"I think it's dope that this a all female tattoo shop." Rome sat behind the receptionist desk.

Ava's shop hadn't opened officially yet. She was still adding things and changing her mind. Her goal was to have the grand opening within the next week. In my opinion it looked nice already, but Ava was on some 'Shopzilla' type shit. Rome was patient enough to deal with it though because she was always high.

"My shops in New York are the same way." Ava's heels clicked against the wooden floor as she paced with her phone to her ear. "Women don't get enough credit in the ink industry." She shrugged.

I nodded.

"Yes, this is Ava Lane. I'm Rajon's step mother." She looked at the time on her Rollie.

And I thought my shit was icy...

"Yes, I got a message saying he wasn't feeling good." She paused. "Have you called his mother? His father is out of state." Ava frowned.

"What's wrong with Rajon?" Rome looked up from her phone. I'm not sure if it was her personal or work since Ava gifted her with a new iPhone.

"Okay, I'm on my way." She hung up the phone and started for the spiral stares. "I need to get my coat. Shit..." she stopped and faced Rome. "Cancel the meeting with the caterer."

Rome nodded. "What day do you wanna reschedule for?"

"Shoot for tomorrow. Early in the morning, I'll just wake up and drop Rajon off with Sadee."

"Okay."

"I know she's probably tired of me canceling. She gon' fuck around and flake on me, yo." Her thick New York accent was funny when she was mad. "That shit is bad for business." She started up the stairs. "I'ma taze Leah's ass."

Me and Rome laughed. Leah was Roman's baby mama. Her and Ava only got a long sometimes. *Most* of the time they were at each other's necks. Ava seemed like more of a mother to Rajon in my opinion.

"She gon' mess around and really taze Leah one day." Rome chuckled tapping her phone. "Leah try her every other day."

I chuckled.

"Ro, I'm on my way to get Rajon from school." Ava hit the landing of the stairs slipping her left arm into her peacoat. "I'm taking him home. I'll just work from there." She switched her phone to her other ear and put her coat on fully. "Hold on, baby. Rome y'all can chill here, but don't forget to lock up." She pointed.

Rome nodded. "Kiss Rajon for me."

Ava walked out of the shop still talking on the phone.

"I bet it's cool as hell working with Ava."

"It is." I listened as she spoke to the caterer apologizing for Ava. She swore that if they still wanted to do business, Ava wouldn't cancel again and if she did, she'd pay the full price.

Drake: *Wassup? Is you sitting on my face all weekend or what?*

I laughed.

Me: *Is that how you start a conversation?*

"Thank you. She'll see you tomorrow at nine." Rome hung up the phone. "I swear Ava don't take a day off."

"How ya know she gon' pay full price? What if something else comes up?"

"Then I'll pay out of my own pocket." Rome shrugged. "The woman sounded a little aggravated. They were supposed to meet in thirty minutes."

Drake: *Answer the question, kid*

Me: *Stop calling me that*

"Does Royal ever take a hit at your age?" I stood up and walked to the receptionist counter. Leaning on my elbows I waited for her to answer.

"No."

"Drake does. He calls me 'kid'."

"Maybe it's a pet name." She shrugged.

"Ain't shit *kiddish* about me, though. I sure wasn't fuckin' him like a kid. I was on my grown woman shit."

Rome laughed.

"It had to be fire cause his ass won't leave me alone." I smiled.

"How old is Drake again?"

"Twenty-six."

"He is only a couple years older than Royal. I guess Drake looks more mature because of his time in prison."

"I told him I wanna take it slow. All this shit going on with Tate got me looking at niggas funny. I still can't believe he did that shit."

"I'm just happy you're done with his funny style ass."

"You and me both, sis." I grabbed a chocolate out of the candy jar. "I don't wanna have sex with Drake because apparently sex clouds my judgment."

"You preaching to the choir." Rome sat her phone down. "Myka is three months pregnant and my dumb ass is still playing house."

"You gotta do better." I chuckled, and Rome rolled her eyes. "I like Royal. He gets you out the house."

"I like Royal too. He listens to me."

I smiled. "Erin said when he came to the house, Roman and Tone were on his head. She was going through all the cameras in the house when she saw them all standing on the porch."

I nodded. "She came and got me. That's how I knew to come down."

"And Tone talked to him?"

"More like threatened him."

"At least your brother is taking interest in your life. Mine is salty right now cause I didn't wanna watch his kids at his house." I did not like his baby mama, Sasha. She used to be Erin's best-friend, but they fell out not too long ago.

"We should make drinks at Royal's tonight." Rome broke the silence. "His bar is full of shit we can mix up." She pushed back from the counter and stood up.

"I'm down." I went to grab my things.

Drake: *I'ma see you later, kid*

ROME

"Is it okay if I invite Erica over?"

"I don't care. Hold on." Royal told me and then the phone hung up.

Frowning, I dropped down onto the couch. It was going on nine and I hadn't seen Royal all day. After removing a pre-rolled swisher from the foil packet, I lit the blunt and put it to my lips. Since Erica was coming over, I figured we could get drunk and watch movies. I wasn't into the party scene and Erica had fallen back too.

Royal called back just as I exhaled. "Yeah."

"Aye, Rome, Myka is on her way over there to get Misa's iPad."

Man...

"I told her not be on no bullshit."

"Royal..."

"Rome, do this for me, a'ight? She should be pulling up in a minute. Let me call you back, shorty." He rushed me off the phone and ended the call.

Getting up from my seat, I headed for the bar. "Alexa..." I inhaled deeply and then exhaled slowly. "Play, 'Challenger' by The Dream".

Once behind the bar, I poured me a shot of Patron. Tossing it back quickly, I took another long hit from my blunt before putting it out. Hearing the doorbell made me roll my eyes.

Rome be the bigger the person.

I had to coach myself as I climbed the steps to the second level of Royal's townhouse. With my arms crossed I moved slowly to the front door. Myka's index finger must've been glued to the doorbell. When I snatched the door open, she mugged me. I unlocked the glass screen door.

"Did Royal call you?"

"Mhm." I led the way back inside. "He said Misa left her iPad."

Myka looked me up and down. "Well, where is it?"

I mugged her back. "I don't know, call Royal and ask him."

She chuckled before leaving the living room. Taking a seat on the sectional, I waited for Myka to get what she needed and leave. Erica was on her way, and she hated Myka.

"Tell Royal, Misa wants to come over this weekend."

I titled my head in confusion. "Why can't you?"

"Ain't that your man?"

"What does that have to do with you telling him Misa wants to come over?" Myka was being petty. The only problem with that was, I wasn't the petty type. Why waste my time and energy?

She shrugged. "This is your house too, right? I mean he let you be here without him. Royal don't usually let bitches post up in his home without him." She smiled.

"Myka..." I crossed my arms. "Let's get a clear understanding before you leave."

Her perfectly arched, right eyebrow rose.

"What me and Royal got going on, ain't got shit to do with you. What you and him do with Misa ain't none of my business either."

Myka rubbed her hand across her stomach. "Did he tell you I was pregnant?" She smirked.

"He sure did."

Her smile dropped.

"Three months, congratulations." I walked past her. "Did you get everything you needed?"

Myka trying to throw her pregnancy in my face didn't move me. She wanted a reaction from me but I didn't have one to give her. I'd planned on having me and Erica's drinks already made before she came, Myka was fuckin' up my vibe. She was having Royal's baby... good for her. She had to be tied to the nigga for life, not me.

I liked Royal ... a lot, but it wasn't that deep. We were both still learning, still growing, still trying to figure out life. That alone was enough pressure to stress a person out. So, I wasn't about to trip off Myka and her two kids. They were Royal's problem, not mine.

Don't get me wrong, I would never treat his kids bad, but they weren't my priority. They were his. I knew what I was getting myself into, though. If me and Royal went the distance, Myka would always be a problem. I was willing to show her respect, until she gave me a reason to show my ass.

"Yeah, I got everything." She answered my question as we came up on the door. When I pulled it open, Erica was on the other side. Myka opened the screen door. "Who are you?"

Erica smacked her lips. "Baby mama today is the day."

I chuckled.

"Rome gotta put up with you, I don't." She bumped Myka as she stepped into the house and walked past me.

"Royal know you got people in his house?"

"Bye, Myka." I waved before shutting the door in her face.

I found Erica sitting at the bar, helping herself to a mint. "What was she doing here?"

"Getting Misa's iPad." I went behind the bar. "Dark or light? I was thinking we try to make 'Pink Panties'." Drinking wasn't really my thing, but I was in a safe place, and I knew my two drink limit.

Erica nodded. "So, you're really okay with Myka being pregnant?"

"As long as Myka stays in her lane, I'll stay in mine." I headed for the kitchen to get the blender.

DRAKE

"What you 'bouta get into?" I hung out of my driver's window and locked B's with Royal.

His eyes surfed the semi crowded block. "Shit stop at the crib real quick. Rome and Erica over there getting drunk and shit."

Hearing Erica was at his house peaked my interest. "Ah, yeah."

Royal shook his head at me knowingly. "Yeah, Rome texted me talking 'bout they bouta go get something to eat, I told her hard-headed ass to stay put."

I looked through my review mirror. "I'ma just follow you over there."

"Shorty got it like that?" He backed away from my door and looked up the street. "Ole sensitive ass nigga..." Royal tossed his chin up to a red Charger that passed by us and then we watched it until it left the block.

I chuckled, rolling my window up.

∽

When I backed into Royal's driveway, I grabbed my phone from the cup holder. Calling Erica, I let my seat back. We hadn't talked all day, but that didn't mean she wasn't on my mind. I didn't want to start a conversation with her through text and then be ghost during most of it. She was always by her phone, so she always hit me right back. I didn't have time for all that.

"Hello?"

"Come here."

"Where is here?"

"Outside."

The phone went silent for a few seconds.

"Okay." She said and then told Rome, not to 'judge her life'. They shared a laugh and then she hung up the phone.

I watched Erica has she exited the house and descended the steps. She flipped the furry hood to her coat over her head and then stopped to bend down and fix the bottom of her jeans. When she finally did get to the passenger's side, I popped the locks. The door swung open and cold air filled my whip almost instantly.

"Hey, Drake." She smiled hopping inside.

"Wassup, kid." I turned the lights over our head on so I could look her over. She'd gone all out on her makeup. It didn't matter to me whether Erica wore makeup or not. I knew what she looked like both ways. And she was dope as fuck; the makeup only enhanced it.

Erica shook her head and the bamboo earrings in her ears dangled. "Nothing for real. School and work. The usual."

"How was that?"

She shrugged. "Okay, I guess. I'm just ready to graduate."

"When is that?"

"May...thank God." She looked out of her window. "School don't even feel the same." I chuckled, and she faced me frowning. "What's funny?"

"You, man." I drawled. "You and these little high school ass problems."

Erica leaned on the arm rest. "I'm eighteen, Drake."

"I know that, *Erica*." I licked my lips.

"And I'm in *high school*."

I shrugged, then looked out of my rearview mirror.

"Can you be a little more sympathetic?" Her voice softened. "Every time I tell you how I'm feeling you make me feel worse by saying I shouldn't feel how I feel." She rambled. "It's been a rough couple of weeks for me." Erica stared at me.

"All I'm tryna do is make you stop all this sappy shit."

Her faced dropped. "You are so rude."

"You sad over a bum and the fact that your school knows you give some sloppy toppy."

Erica punched my arm, laughing. "Drake!" She laughed harder. "That's not funny."

Shrugging, I pressed ignore when my phone started ringing.

"I'm going to be known as that girl in school who sucked dick."

"Publicly." I corrected, and she smacked her lips. "You got too much to be grateful for to be beatin' yourself up over nothing." When she sneezed I turned the heat up. "Bless you."

"Thank you." She sniffled.

"You need to be focused on what you gon' do after graduation. 'Cause that's the shit that's gon' determine how successful you are in the future, not this shit."

After a little thought, she adjusted her seat. "I guess you're right."

"You guess?"

She sighed. "I wanna go to school out of state."

"Do that then. I'll come see you every weekend."

Erica smiled, and I knew exactly why I was drawn to her. It was her smile, it wasn't forced or fake. You could see it in her eyes and in feel in her body language. "You serious?"

I nodded, and she cheesed harder.

"That's sweet, Drake."

"I do what I can." Not only that, but I was willingly to do whatever Erica wanted. Don't ask me why, 'cause I couldn't tell you. I just was...

I was a street nigga, and Erica was a good girl. She still had a lot of life to enjoy before she settled down with a nigga like me. And I wasn't ready to settle down yet. But the magnetic pull she had on me was indescribable. Even though we couldn't be together right now, Erica was going be my wife later.

ROYAL

"Yo ass drunk." I picked Rome up and sat her down on the bar. "What you been drinking?"

She shrugged. "A little bit of this and that."

I pulled her bottom lip into my mouth and tasted the Patron on her. Gripping her ass, I lifted her off the bar.

"Don't drop me, Royal." She panicked.

I frowned. "Drop you?"

Rome wrapped her arms around my neck. "I done gained a little weight."

Shaking my head, I sat her back down on the bar. "Come up outta that."

She looked confused. "Out of what? My clothes?"

I nodded take my coat off and then pulling my hoodie over my head. After dropping both on the floor, I undid my pants.

Rome laughed. "Baby, really?"

I didn't have long, I had shit to do. Romie Rome wanted some foreplay, but we didn't have time for all that. As I pulled at her leggings and panties, she removed her shirt. After tossing her clothes, I unfastened her bra.

"Royal, what if Erica comes in here?" Rome moaned a little when my tongue slid over her nipples. She shuddered when I slipped my middle finger in her and sucked on her neck. "Mmmm."

My dick started swelling at just the thought of Rome's juices running down my balls. When she grabbed both sides of my face for a kiss, I picked her up as I stuck my tongue in her mouth for a sloppy kiss. I slid Rome down the length of my dick. When I hit the bottom, she held onto me tighter. Our kiss deepened as I gripped both of her ass cheeks and started pounding the pussy.

"*Rome...*" Rome whispered. "Baby."

I bit down on my bottom lip. Every time I pulled back a little, her pussy sucked me right back in like a vacuum. "Damn..."

I went harder.

"Ummm...uhn... *yes.*" She panted. "Right there, Daddy."

I gripped her ass cheeks tighter and let her fuck me back a little. She worked her hips in a circular motion while she sucked on my neck.

Fuck.

I held Rome tighter as she slithered her body like a snake. When she started fucking me harder, I had to take back control. The real nigga in me wouldn't ever let Rome out fuck me, the freak in me though... I had to remind myself we didn't have time for all that. She had to be drunk, cause Rome never fucked like this, she usually wanted that gentle shit.

Okay, so shorty got some savage in her.

Taking back control, I slid her all the way to my tip and then slammed her back down hard. Rome whimpered into my mouth each time I did that.

"I'm comin'..." she sighed. "Keep it right there." When her head fell back, I sucked down hard on the front of her neck. "Mmmm, Royal..."

"Fuck Rome." I slowed down and bounced her on the tip of my dick.

"*Fuuccck.*" Her body jerked as she held onto me tight. "*Fuck.*"

"I'm bouta bust." Biting down on the corner of my lip, I slid her all the way down my shaft and then hurriedly pulled out. My nut shot all on her stomach and lower chest. "Fuck."

∼

"I'll be back to pick you up for breakfast." I said over my shoulder as I tied my wheat Timbs. "I ain't seen Misa in a few days.

Rome sat down on the bed. "Okay."

I probably wasn't the best father, but I loved my daughter. She was why I went so hard. Did I feel bad about not seeing her some days? Fuck yeah. Misa was a little girl. She needed a full-time father.

But I couldn't be full time and provide for her. So sometimes Daddy forgot to call and tell her he loved her. That didn't mean I didn't. She was on my mind twenty-four-seven, but sadly, I couldn't let that consume me. I had a bag to get so she could be whatever she wanted in life.

Then there was Rome. She needed just as much time and attention, but I only seen her maybe in the morning before work, or at night when I could spare a couple hours. That's why I wanted her here with me. Even if that meant she had to bring that ugly ass dog. The dog provided a common ground for Misa and Rome, so she was good with me.

"Or... I could just cook breakfast here." She offered with a shrug. "We have eggs, bacon, pancake mix, and pretty much everything else."

I frowned. "Since when?" Grocery shopping was probably at the bottom of my to do list.

"I noticed breakfast is where you and Misa get to catch up." The cotton robe she had on was swallowing her slim frame. "So, every time I was out running errands, I would get things for here." She crawled over to me.

"'Preciate it."

She shrugged. "No problem. So, breakfast here? Then maybe you could lay down for a minute? Grizzy B hasn't been to the dog park in a minute."

Rome had been trying to get me to agree to let her take Misa with her to the dog park. I wasn't trying to push my kids off on Rome, but she was holding me down. I kept telling her wait until I had time to go with them, but a nigga was always busy. I trusted Rome with Misa, and I trusted Misa's judgement in people. Rome was the truth.

"A'ight." My answer must've thrown her off because she perked up.

"Really?"

"Yeah." I stood up and fixed my jeans.

She climbed off the bed. "Be safe, okay?" Rome's eyes bored into mine. She was still caught up on me getting shot. Bullet wounds heal, the money didn't stop.

"I'll be back." I licked my lips and then kissed her. I led the way back downstairs just as Erica was coming through the front door.

"That's gone be my husband...watch." She shook her head smiling as she walked past the bannister, tugging gently at the iced out tennis necklace around her neck.

EPILOGUE

YOU'RE FOREVER IN MY HEART.

Erica rushed to put on the finishing touches to her outfit. She was always the last person to be ready. Drake was outside waiting on her, but she refused to leave the house without making sure her wardrobe and hair were straight. She was supposed to have been gone thirty minutes ago if she wanted to be on time. In her defense, Drake had been M.I.A the entire day until the last minute.

She didn't understand how he could always be near his phone but take forever to get back to her. When they were together his phone was ringing nonstop. Seeing that he barely had time for her was enough to help her not fall head over heels in love. Drake was fresh out prison and on a money mission. Every day he proved to Erica didn't have time to fall in love.

So why should she?

After grabbing her purse, Erica left her bedroom, spraying herself down with perfume. She was currently the only one in the Morris Mansion and that had been her biggest fear. Not because their home was massive, and she was alone, but because that meant everybody was going to be looking for her. When Erin was leaving, she promised to leave in a timely manner. Unfortunately, she chose to change her outfit a few times before she decided what to wear.

Erica stepped into the night air and hurried to Drake's G-wagon. Once she was inside and the door was closed, she shivered from the cold. "Hey, Drake." She smiled. It didn't matter how much they talked on the phone or FaceTimed, being in his presence was a whole different experience.

"Wassup, kid." Drake gripped her chin gently and swiped slowly.

Erica loved when he did that. "What you do today?" She asked pulling her seat belt across her body and then securing the buckle.

"Shit..." Before he pulled away from the curb, he glanced at her. "You over there lookin real icy, shorty."

She laughed. "I'm just tryna keep up with you." Erica looked Drake over slowly. As usual, he was dressed in all black. The chains around his neck, just like the watch on his wrist were sparkling.

Drake drove off the compound with Erica recording a video on Snapchat. He didn't understand what the hype was. Nobody in their right mind wanted random people to know what they were doing all day every day. But Erica jumped from social site to social site giving daily updates on her life. You would think she was a celebrity.

After thinking it over, Drake guessed in a way she was. Tate's bitch move was still haunting her social life, but at least she wasn't whining and complaining anymore.

"Rome just texted me." Erica tapped her phone. "She said Sadee isn't there yet, so we're still making good timing."

Drake shook his head. By the time they got to Ava's grand opening, the party would be in full swing. This was why he tried to get her to spend the night with him the night before. The Morris Manson was too far away from the city to be making last minute trips. He tried to tell Erica that but she was bull headed and insisted on staying home so she could finish her vision board.

"I told her to make a video just in case I miss it. That way I can still post it to my story."

"You a social media junky, Erica." Drake rested his right arm on her headrest.

"And you're a criminal, *Drake*." Erica shot back, giving him the side eye. He had some nerve to judge her. At least her past time didn't consist of her harming other human beings and doing illegal things.

Drake chuckled. "Touché..."

"You should make you a Snapchat. And I'll oversee it." She snapped a picture.

Frowning, Drake flew through a green light. "Why would you be in charge of my page?"

"So, I can post pictures of me. That why these chicks know, even though we aren't together, I'm número uno." Erica started a video. "Ain't that right, baby?" She smiled for the camera before putting it on Drake.

He nodded.

"You gotta say wassup to my Snapchat fam."

"Fuck your Snapchat fam." He said coolly.

Erica laughed as she ended the video. "I'm posting that too." After she captioned the video 'Pray for Drake', she added it to her story. "I can't wait to see how this tattoo shop comes out."

Erica dropped her phone in her lap. For weeks Rome had been running herself ragged to make sure everything came out just right. Ava was a perfectionist and she'd rubbed off on poor Rome.

"I know it's gone be dope."

Erica nodded in agreement. "Roman bossed up getting her that space for Valentine's Day. That's what you call hubby goals."

Drake glanced at her. "That's all I gotta do? By you a store front?" If he would've known that was all he needed to do, they could skip Ava's grand opening and go look for a space right then.

Smiling, Erica pulled her visor down to inspect her lipstick. This was her first-time rocking purple, but surprisingly it came out okay. Not her favorite, but doable. "No, that ain't my thing." She examined her eyelashes.

Drake turned the music up a little. "What's your *thing*?"

Erica closed the visor after she was satisfied with her once over. "Ice, baby." She cheesed, and he chuckled at her.

They rode in content for a while both lost in their thoughts. Since agreeing they would move at a slower pace, a genuine friendship was blossoming between the duo. Though both were hot-headed and outspoken individuals, they found a common ground in being patient with one another. Deep down they felt like they were destined to be together. But they were both intelligent enough to give it time to work itself out.

Erica picked her phone back up and got back on her Snapchat.

"Ice me out, nigga ...Ice me out." She sung acapella as she flexed in the camera.

∽

ROME LAUGHED as Ava playfully talked shit to Erica about being late to her grand opening. Only Erica. It wasn't like she'd woke up late or started getting ready last either. If memory served Rome right, Erica was usually the first person in the house up. Not only that, but when she'd left the compound early, Erica had already started getting dressed.

Now how was she late? Rome didn't have that answer. She and Drake waltzed in smiling like they didn't have a care in the world.

"Now that everybody is here." Ava looked back and forth between Drake and Erica, gaining a few laughs. "I just wanna thank y'all for coming out and supporting me. Roman knows how much my shops in New York meant to me." She glanced at Roman.

He tipped his glass to her.

"I'm not going to give a long speech, cause I know some of y'all wanna get tatted." Ava's eyes skipped across each person in the room. Her confidence was so loud, if Rome didn't know Ava on a personal level, she might've been intimated by her. "I wanna thank my sister-in-law Rome, for putting up with my crazy ways and delivering." She gave a slight nod to Rome.

Rome respected that, because working for Ava was a different ball game. Between her brashness and highly obnoxious ways, Rome came to work some days not knowing which Ava she was going to get.

However, she'd figured out the science of working for Ava Lane. Go with the flow. Nothing about Ava's life was repetitive.

They were the perfect work match. All Rome's life, she'd gone with the flow of things. At least Ava gave her space to be herself. She never hassled her because she trusted Rome to get things done. Which was why this grand opening was almost as important to Rome as it was Ava.

After she was done thanking everyone for coming out, the party went back into full swing. Rome's eyes surfed the crowd and when they landed on Royal, his were already on her. She watched as he made his way toward her and started to meet him halfway.

"Rome." Hearing Ava's voice stopped her mid-stride.

She faced her.

"Everything came out perfect. I really do appreciate you stepping up." There were days when Ava wasn't even in the same state, but Rome's work never stopped. Ava paid close attention to Rome and how she handled working under pressure. Ava saw a lot of herself in Rome.

"No problem. Thanks for trusting me with your baby." They shared a genuine laugh as Royal approached.

"I want you know this is just as much your baby as it mine." And Ava meant that sincerely. She'd planned on opening a shop in Kansas City, but not this soon. Her work load was over flowing but having Rome around relieved some of her stress. "Which is why, you'll be shop manager."

Rome's smiled widened. "Really? I thought you wanted shop manager to have a degree."

Ava nodded. "I do... Which is why I want you to go to school part time." Ava's eyes danced around Rome's face. She couldn't help but look out for Rome in a big sister kind of way. Ava saw great potential in Rome, she was just lost trying to find where she belonged.

Rome had given school a lot of thought over the past couple of weeks; especially after her conversation with Tone. This wasn't the first time Ava had brought it up to her neither. She figured she could obtain a degree in business and start from there. "I can do that." Rome nodded.

"Bet." Ava smiled before walking off.

"I'm proud of you, Romie Rome." Royal pulled her into a hug.

Rome quickly looked around the room for her brothers but didn't see them. "Are you trying to get us killed?" She laughed and he shrugged.

"I can't show my woman affection?" Royal planted a soft kiss on her lips. "Let her know how sexy she lookin' in this dress?" He gave both of her ass cheeks a firm squeeze.

Rome's cheeks flushed. "Royal ... you got people looking at us."

Again, he shrugged.

"You know your brother is on his way down here? Right?" Erica came up on the side of the duo with their niece, Toni, on her hip.

Rome chuckled as she pulled away and put a little distance between them. She already knew which brother Erica was referring to; Roman. He let it be known he didn't approve of Royal and Rome showing public display's of attention. If they kissed in front of him, he'd smack in his lips in irritation. Earlier that week he'd walked out of the room when he felt like Royal hugged her too long when he dropped her off at work.

Erica walked away laughing.

"You wanna get a tattoo?" She asked Royal who scanned the room quickly.

He shrugged, and she led the way to one of the fancy booths in the back of the shop. With no budget, she and Ava had gone all out. The entire shop was done in silver, black and white. The receptionist's desk had a built-in fish tank, and the waiting area looked like a hookah bar. Chandelier's hung in each artist's booth and they all had matching pink, leather tables and chairs.

It was dope and Rome was psyched that she would be the one managing it. If you would've told her this would be her life three months ago, Rome probably would've laughed in your face. They stepped in Tai's booth. She was the only artist Rome was willing to give her money to because she was the best in her opinion. Rome had seen each employee's portfolio and Tai's work was the only one who's photos wowed her.

"Hey, Rome," Tai sat in her chair texting. "You getting some ink?"

Rome nodded. "Yep just something on our fingers."

Royal frowned. "I ain't got space on my hands." He held his tatted hands up.

"The inside." Rome sat down. "In the inside of our ring fingers."

Royal gave her an uneasy look. "What we getting there?"

"Two-fourteen." Rome watched as Tai got everything ready.

"Why that?" When Royal agreed to be her plus one, he didn't count on getting matching tattoos. He hadn't even known Rome that long. He didn't even have Myka's name tatted on him and she'd given him a daughter.

"Valentine's Day." Rome laughed at his apprehension. "The day you asked me to be yours." She shook her head.

Royal nodded. He could do that. Valentine's day brought him and Rome closer and made their relationship official. He was willing to honor that if that's what Rome wanted. She had stepped up for him in a major way by accepting his kids and rocking with him despite the slip up with his baby mama. What better way to show his appreciation?

As he watched Tai start on Rome's finger, he kissed the top of her head.

"Thank you for being mine."

THE END

Want to be notified when the new, hot Urban Fiction and Interracial Romance books are released? Text the keyword "JWP" to 22828 to receive an email notifying you of new releases, giveaways, announcements, and more!

Jessica Watkins Presents is the home of many well-known, best-selling authors in Urban Fiction and Interracial Romance. We provide editing services, promotion and marketing, one-on-one consulting with a renowned, national best-selling author, assistance in branding, and more, FREE of charge to you, the author.
We are currently accepting submissions for the following genres: Urban Fiction/Romance, Interracial Romance, and Interracial/Paranormal Romance. If you are interested in becoming a best-selling author and have a FINISHED manuscript, please send the synopsis, genre and the first three chapters in a PDF or Word file to jwp.submissions@gmail.com. Complete manuscripts must be at least 45,000 words.Tag a friend or family member who you know needs to be a published author!

Made in the USA
Coppell, TX
14 June 2024